Under the Bridge

Under the Bridge

ELLEN KINDT McKENZIE

HENRY HOLT AND COMPANY
NEW YORK

To the memory of my brother,
Orin Hill Kindt

Henry Holt and Company, Inc.
Publishers since 1866
115 West 18th Street
New York, New York 10011

Henry Holt is a registered
trademark of Henry Holt and Company, Inc.

Copyright © 1994 by Ellen Kindt McKenzie
All rights reserved.
Published in Canada by Fitzhenry & Whiteside Ltd.,
195 Allstate Parkway, Markham, Ontario L3R 4T8.

Library of Congress Cataloging-in-Publication Data
McKenzie, Ellen Kindt.
    Under the bridge / Ellen Kindt McKenzie.   p.   cm.
    Summary: When Ritchie's younger sister, Rosie, gets very sick
after their mother suddenly goes away, Rosie begins to receive
letters from a lonely troll, and these letters help Ritchie cope
with his mother's absence, his father's seeming indifference,
and the fifth-grade class bully.
    [1. Brothers and sisters—Fiction.   2. Parent and child—Fiction.
3. Trolls—Fiction.   4. Bullies—Fiction.]   I. Title.
PZ7.M478676Un   1994   [Fic]—dc20   94-3415

ISBN 0-8050-3398-X

First Edition—1994
Designed by Christy Hale
Printed in the United States of America
on acid-free paper. ∞
10   9   8   7   6   5   4   3   2   1

Under the Bridge

One

It happened so fast. One day everything was the way it should be. The next day it was different. All wrong.

The evening before our mother was gone was like any evening. I was lying on the living-room floor reading the instructions for my model airplane while our mother read "The Three Billy Goats Gruff" to Rosie. Rosie loved that story and she asked for it at least once a week. I was too old for it, so I pretended I wasn't listening, but I did listen because I liked it too. There was something about big Billy Goat Gruff butting the troll off the bridge that made me feel good.

This night, after our mother finished the book, Rosie said, "The troll lives under Mr. Grailowsky's bridge now, doesn't he?"

Thad Grailowsky lived at the other end of the field behind us, where Kohler Creek came out from Ornabeck's

Woods. The creek ran through his orchard—that's where the bridge was—down to the road and under it.

Our mother almost smiled. "If he does, I've never seen him."

"Maybe that's because Mr. Grailowsky doesn't have billy goats. Only chickens," Rosie said.

"Maybe," our mother said. She took a deep breath and blew on Rosie's neck and made her laugh and squirm. Rosie's laugh always made everybody laugh. Except my father.

My father looked up from the newspaper. The headlines were about Germany and Poland and Russia.

"Do you have to make so much noise?" he asked.

Our mother got up. She wasn't almost smiling anymore. Her mouth was tight. It was that way most of the time now. It made me feel bad. She used to laugh a lot too, like Rosie, but it seemed like my father didn't want her to—as if it bothered him, the way everything I did bothered him.

Our mother took Rosie upstairs to see that she brushed her teeth before she went to bed. She came back downstairs and sat down and started darning socks. Her mouth was tighter than I'd ever seen it. My father finished reading the paper and turned on the radio. William Shirer was talking about President Roosevelt and then about how the Maginot Line protected France. After a while my father told me to go to bed. I started to pick up my stuff from the living-room floor.

"Hurry up," he said.

I *was* hurrying. Couldn't he see I had to be careful not to break the balsa-wood sticks?

4

My mother said, "Good night, Ritchie."

Usually she came upstairs later and told me to stop reading and turn off the light. Then she'd take my glasses off and set them on the lamp stand. She'd kiss me good night and turn off the light herself. If my father had come up too, sometimes I'd hear him say,

"Don't do that. He's too old to kiss good night."

This night she didn't come up. I turned the light off myself.

I woke up and lay on my back, listening. I didn't know what woke me, but I heard voices and wondered who was visiting. Except for Aunt Vickie and Uncle Len, people didn't visit us. Once a month, on Sunday afternoon, Aunt Vickie, she's my father's sister—my mother didn't have any sisters or brothers—Aunt Vickie and Uncle Len would come over with our cousins. Our mother always figured out something special for us to do. Mary Alice and Margaret and Patsy would play with Rosie. But Len Junior and Gordy and I—they called me twerp—always got into some kind of trouble, no matter what our mother had planned. We threw mud clods at the house or ran through poison ivy or fell in the creek or went through the woods to the quarry where we weren't supposed to go because it was dangerous. This month we'd stolen apples from Thad Grailowsky's orchard. It was easy to do that because there was a path alongside the creek from the bridge out of his orchard back to the woods.

I always said what we did was my idea because once I'd told on Len Junior, and my father got mad and said, "Don't be a tattletale."

It didn't much matter. We all got it the same when we'd done something wrong.

But I knew Aunt Vickie wasn't there that night. Her voice is loud and she talks steady without ever giving anybody else a chance.

I stared at the ceiling. A red light and then a white light kept flashing there. My whole body was still, as if it was holding its breath, but I couldn't tell what anybody was saying. Then I heard car doors close. A car started up and the lights went away. I listened until the whole sound of it was gone. I kept listening, but all I heard was the sound of the switch engines in the train yard, the chuffing and hissing and the clatter the boxcars make when they jerk apart as the train starts or push together when it stops. Almost three miles away that was, but when the wind was in the southeast you could hear them all night long. Once I heard the other train at the grade crossing not so far from us—the North Shore that ran every hour between Chicago and Milwaukee. Sometimes I'd hear a car coming. The lights from it would move across the ceiling and then be gone.

My father woke me up in the morning.

"Why aren't you up? You'll be late," he said.

I knew that because I heard the milkman's horse on the street before he finished saying it.

When I went downstairs, our mother wasn't there. Rosie was sitting in her high chair. She could sit in a regular chair, but she's small for four years old, so when she did that, her chin came just to the edge of the table. It was easier for her to use the high chair. She was still in her pajamas. She was crying and licking the tears off the corners of her mouth. Her nose was running.

"Where's Mama?" I asked.

"Your mother's sick," my father said. "They took her to the hospital. Keep still, Rosie."

I wanted to ask how sick, what kind of sick? But I couldn't. My father hardly ever answered my questions. He hardly ever looked at me, so what was the use? Even so, I kept asking inside. What made her sick? Say something. But he didn't look at me. He didn't tell me.

I had to wipe Rosie's nose. I couldn't stand looking at it. I guess I pinched it too hard, but I wasn't used to wiping her nose. I gave her the big cotton handkerchief to do it herself. Then I got down a bowl for me, and Rosie's special one with the alphabet around the edge. I put cornflakes in both bowls and sprinkled on some sugar. I shook the milk bottle to mix the cream in and poured milk over the cornflakes. I gave Rosie her little spoon. She could have used a big one, but she liked the little one.

Rosie started eating, but I had such a hard rock in my stomach I didn't think I could swallow without throwing up.

"What about Rosie?" I asked. "What's she going to do by herself?"

"I'm taking her to Vickie's for today. Eat your breakfast and go to school," my father said.

That made me feel better. If Aunt Vickie was taking care of Rosie for today, that must mean our mother would be back tomorrow.

But I wished I'd only taken half as many cornflakes. I

couldn't eat them all. If my father had let me have a dog, I could have given the leftover mush to the dog.

"I'll be late," I said, and got up, put my bowl in the sink, and ran to get my jacket. My father didn't look at me. He didn't even say "Um" with his mouth closed. He'd find half a bowl of cornflakes in the sink, but I'd be almost at school by then.

Everything on the way to school was clear that day, as if it was waiting in an awful kind of way—the house, the sky, the whole street.

We live on the north edge of town, where the houses are far apart. Today our house looked alone the way I'd never noticed, a tall gray box with half a block of field on both sides of it and a whole block of field behind it. Steps go up to the front and back doors, but there aren't any porches with rails, just landings.

There's a bridal-wreath bush on one side of the front steps. In the summer the bush has lots of little white flowers with brown in the middle. They don't smell very good.

When I went down the front steps, I saw Rosie's tricycle—it used to be mine—lying on its side in the bush. I noticed how faded and chipped off the red paint was. There were some iris leaves mashed under it. The flowers had been purple, only now they were dried up and looked like gray tissue paper. Even the stalks were white and dry. Iris was all the flowers we had. Oh, and some hollyhocks by the back door. They'd gone to seed.

Our house didn't have any trees.

I looked across the field behind us toward Thad

Grailowsky's shack. It had a big maple tree in the front yard. You could see the top of it over his roof. There were flowers all around the shack, even in September. It had a vegetable garden behind it and the apple orchard beside it. There were other trees along the creek—willows and poplars and elms and things. A willow tree near the bridge had started to turn yellow.

Across the street from his shack it was country. Cabbage and onion fields. There was nothing growing there now, just lumpy black dirt waiting for winter.

I walked backward for a minute so I could look at our house again. Maybe our mother was really upstairs changing the beds. Maybe she would be shaking out a blanket over the side of the back steps. Maybe she would wave to me. But the house stayed all alone. The downstairs windows looked black and empty. The upstairs windows looked like small square eyes that didn't see anything.

All of that was clear like never before. All the way to school the houses and trees and fields were clear like never before. Different.

Inside school wasn't clear at all. I kept thinking other things, but not the way I liked to do, like King Arthur and dragons or musketeers or cowboy stuff. This was different. It wasn't pretending something keen. It was just strange—like long division when we had 22 goes into 736. All I could think was, 22 whats go into 736 whats? Do 22 people go into 736 doors? How could they? Would you send them in and out and in and out? What had 736 doors anyway, the Empire State Building in New York? Then I started wondering how many doors it did have. The tallest building in the world! You could lose Melvin Collins in the Empire State Building and never find him again! Would I like to do that!

Melvin Collins is bigger than anybody else in the fifth grade because he got kept back. It was worse for me than anybody because I'm the smallest. I'd got put ahead. He caught me after school again last Wednesday. He got me with a lock hold, wrapped a leg around mine, and pushed me down. Hard. I was lucky I didn't break my glasses.

I wished I could get even. I wished I could hit him so hard, his head would fly off and roll all the way down to 14th Avenue. His head would be nothing but a . . .

"Richard! Richard Willis! Pay attention! What are you thinking! You're behaving just like Melvin!"

I stared at Miss Goodlatty. Me? Like Melvin Collins?

A voice said, "Melvin Collins's head is a squashed tomato."

I'd read a thing how "his words hung in the air." Well, that's what those words did. Only they didn't just hang there. They bounced off the walls and the ceiling and the floor. Up and down and back and forth. *Melvin Collins's head is a squashed tomato.* And it was my voice that bounced until somebody started to laugh. Then everybody laughed. Miss Goodlatty hit the desk hard with her ruler.

"That's enough!" she snapped. "Richard, come to the board and do the next five long-division problems. The rest of you work on page eleven."

I went to the board. I don't know what I did. I put

numbers above and below. I don't remember if they were right or what.

When we went out for recess, Melvin Collins dug me hard in the back with his fist.

"I'll get you, four-eyes," he whispered. "I'm gonna knock your block off!"

TWO

Melvin Collins didn't get me that day because I ran home after school. I thought maybe our mother would be there, but the house was so empty, it didn't even have air in it, so I sat outside on the porch steps.

It was suppertime when my father brought Rosie home. He didn't bring our mother.

The next morning I asked him if she would be home this afternoon.

"No," he said.

"Will she be home tomorrow?" I asked.

"No. Eat your breakfast and go to school."

Melvin Collins didn't get me until Thursday. He got his arm around my neck and said in my ear, "This isn't the big one. The big one is coming, four-eyes." Then he tripped me.

I hurt, but I didn't cry. Third grade maybe you can cry. Fifth grade you can't. Not with other kids standing around. When I got up, I felt in my pocket to see if my glasses were okay. They were thick and cost a lot. Once, my father had said, "If you break them again, you'll go without." So every day now when the bell rang I snapped them shut in the case and put the case in my pocket so they wouldn't get broken if Melvin Collins pushed me down. They were okay. I put them on after everybody was gone so I could see better on my way home. It was neat how the leaves on the trees jumped apart when I put on my glasses.

That night at supper my father said, "Vickie can't keep Rosie after Monday. Mrs. Cavanaugh will come Monday and Friday. Pearl Suslik is coming the other days." That was a lot for my father to say.

Pearl Suslik came and made the beds and did the dishes and swept the kitchen and brought in the milk from the porch and looked after Rosie. Pearl was sixteen and had to go to vocational school in the afternoon, so she took Rosie home with her after lunch and left her with her mother. My father paid Pearl fifty cents a day and lunch.

I went two blocks around to their house for Rosie after I got out of school. Mrs. Suslik was short and fat and pulled her hair into a bun at the back of her neck. Her face was round and wrinkled. She always said, "She's a good little girl, Ritchie. She don't cry."

At first I was afraid Melvin Collins would come to give me "the big one" while I was taking Rosie home, but after a while I hoped maybe he'd forgotten. I couldn't forget, because I knew he hadn't. I wondered what the big one would be. I'd hold Rosie's hand and think, He wouldn't hurt a *really* little girl. But I wasn't sure.

I hated going home on Pearl's days. The house was always so hollow. Sometimes, so we didn't have to be there much before my father got home from work, I'd take Rosie the long way past Thad Grailowsky's shack.

Thad Grailowsky was an old bachelor—maybe almost as old as my father. Len Junior and Gordy and I didn't trust people that old who lived alone, so we stayed away from him. Aunt Vickie said nobody knew what Thad Grailowsky lived on. He didn't have a real job. "Music lessons," Aunt Vickie would say, and sniff hard. Of course, a lot of people didn't have jobs. They were on relief or the WPA. But Aunt Vickie said Thad Grailowsky wasn't on that, either. All summer he worked in his garden, hoeing or stooped over weeding or picking peas or beans. Sometimes people came to visit him. They had Illinois license plates on their cars. From Chicago, we guessed.

That really made us stay away from him, because Len Junior said, "I'm old enough to know a lot goes on in Chicago, and some of it spills over the state line." Thinking about that gave me goose pimples.

But one time Thad Grailowsky sat across from me on the trolley. The knees of his pants were kind of baggy. He had long strong fingers and the backs of his hands were brown. He wore a sweater. He didn't wear a tie. His forehead had one wrinkle going across it. When I looked at that, I couldn't help looking in his eyes. I was surprised. His eyes weren't mean or mad the way I expected because he was old and kept to himself and had something to do with Chicago. They were friendly dark brown with crinkles at the edges as if he liked to smile. He did smile, and I sort of smiled back and then I looked away quick.

When he stood up to get off the trolley, I was surprised again. He was taller than I expected and not hunched over the least bit the way he was in his garden. He looked strong all over and bounced off the trolley and walked away like he had springs in his shoes. His shoes weren't good like my father's. They were worn down at the heels and you couldn't tell if they'd been brown or black. I don't know how she knew, but Aunt Vickie said Thad Grailowsky never bought any clothes except at the Salvation Army. That didn't really count, though, because a lot of people bought clothes at the Salvation Army, even if they didn't say so.

After that, I wasn't afraid of him. His rooster didn't worry me when it crowed in the morning. To prove I wasn't afraid, sometimes when I walked past his shack with Rosie we even stayed on his side of the street. I was always glad he wasn't in the front yard with Blackie when we did. Blackie was his dog. He was a big old mongrel that slept most of the time in a bare spot in the front yard.

Rosie didn't know about Chicago. She'd stop to say, "Hello, Blackie!" When she did, sometimes the dog would twitch and wake up and then bite hard at the end of his back where his tail started, his legs slipping and kicking. Sometimes he'd look off across the street and woof just once. He wouldn't bother to stand up.

Past Thad Grailowky's shack, we'd cross the culvert.

"Is this the bridge where the troll lives?" Rosie asked the first time we crossed it.

"No," I told her. "The bridge is back that way. This is the culvert. It's a big pipe that goes under the road. There's no branches in it to hold on to. If it rained hard, and the culvert got full, the troll would get washed all the way down to Lake Michigan and drown. Anyway, there's no troll."

We crossed it once after it had rained hard. The water was running fast, muddy brown except where it rolled up against the top of the culvert and turned to dirty frothy white.

"Poor troll," Rosie said.

"Why do you like the troll?" I asked. "He's bad!"

"I don't know if I like him. I just feel sorry for him," she said, but she didn't know why.

Every time we walked that way, Rosie'd try to see the bridge, but the trees were in the way. I wouldn't take her on the path along the creek and through the field to get home. That was too close to Thad Grailowsky's shack. We went the long way around the block. Rosie was always so tired, she'd fall asleep on the floor while we were listening to Little Orphan Annie or Jack Armstrong.

Mrs. Cavanaugh came early and stayed until I got home. She did the washing and the ironing and the big cleaning and started supper. Her cooking never smelled as good as our mother's. Everything was boring.

Weekends weren't fun either. I had to stay with Rosie on Saturday mornings when my father went in the car to do the grocery shopping. Sometimes he'd forget something and look mad. I'd say, "I can go to Kulich's corner store for it." He'd give me a quarter, but he'd never say I could have a penny for bubble gum and a baseball card. I'd bring the change and go to my room to read. I wondered if nothing would ever be right and if the house would be empty forever.

Then one night Rosie started crying. Every night she cried more and more over every little thing. When she cried, she always wanted Mama. One night at supper she burned her tongue on the canned chicken-noodle soup. She started to cry. "I want Mama."

My father lost his temper. "You can't have her, so keep still!"

Everything inside me shriveled up and got hard. Rosie gulped and sniffed and her eyes got big. Tears kept coming down her face but she kept still.

Three

"itchie! Richard Willis! You aren't paying attention!"
Miss Goodlatty was mad about something.

I looked her in the face. If I could keep her eyes looking at my eyes, she wouldn't notice the other book I had inside my social-studies book.

"I didn't hear you," I said, and that was so. How could I when Edmond Dantès had just been put in a sack with a cannonball tied to his feet and thrown off the rocks of the Château d'If into the sea? In spite of the noise of the waves, I'd heard his scream, but I hadn't heard Miss Goodlatty. Now her heels were clicking down the aisle.

"What are you reading?" she asked, and lifted *The Count of Monte Cristo* out of my social-studies book, snapped it shut loud, and clicked back to her desk.

What would I do? It was Sue Kolinsky's father's book!

I'd told Sue Kolinsky about *The Three Musketeers* and *Twenty Years After*, that our mother had and I'd read. She said her father had *The Count of Monte Cristo*, only they couldn't read it because they were Catholic. She lent it to me, and now Miss Goodlatty had it.

Everything turned gray again.

The gray was everywhere. It seemed like it came off the outside of the house and stayed with me. I'd turn the lights on when I got home from school, but the gray came inside. Then it followed me to school and sat on Miss Goodlatty's desk. It even made Miss Goodlatty's questions whispered and gray. That's why I didn't hear them.

The only time the gray didn't bother me was when I was reading a book I liked.

At noon I went to Miss Goodlatty.

"It's Sue Kolinsky's father's book," I said. "Please give it to her. She'll get in trouble and it's not her fault. I won't read it any more in school."

"You certainly won't read anything that you're not supposed to read in school," she said.

She did give Sue the book. She had to, because it had her father's name in it. At least Miss Goodlatty couldn't keep it to read herself. But Sue was scared her father would find out she'd borrowed it, so she took it home.

That night the telephone rang. It was for my father. He listened for a while. Then he hung up.

He didn't say who it was until breakfast. Then he said, "Your teacher called me about you last night. You'd better straighten out."

I didn't want the rest of my cornflakes again. I had to say something. "Can we visit our mother in the hospital?" I asked.

"No," he said. He hadn't told me which hospital she was in—St. Mary's or the city hospital. I thought he must have gone to see her one day last week because he got dressed up, not for the office. He was still dressed up and home sitting in the living room reading the paper when I got back from school with Rosie. I'd waited for him to tell us he'd been to see her, but he didn't. Anyway, where else would he go?

Now I waited again, but he didn't say any more. Just "No." He didn't talk about our mother. Rosie and I didn't talk about her either.

That made two whole days that were bad.

The next day—Wednesday—was worse. At breakfast Rosie threw up all over the floor. At least she didn't ask for Mama. When I got to school, I didn't have a book to read, and then Miss Goodlatty told me she wanted to talk to me at recess.

"You're not doing what you're able to do, Ritchie," she said. "You got put ahead and were still getting good grades. You mustn't let things slide this way."

If everything wasn't already so bad, I wouldn't have said it. But it was, so I said, "Who cares."

That made her mad. She sent me to the office. Miss Mieres, the principal, scolded me for being impertinent and made me sit there through the rest of recess.

Before she sent me back to the room, she said, "We all know your mother's had a nervous breakdown, and we're all sorry about that. But you can't let that ruin your life by stopping you from learning. By this time you should realize you have to pick up the pieces and do your work. Now go back and behave yourself. We only want to help you."

The only thing I really paid attention to were her words that my mother had had a "nervous breakdown." So *that* was why she was in the hospital all this time. But what was a nervous breakdown? Who were "we" that "we all know." *I* didn't know! My father had never told *me*! My father had never told anybody that I knew about. Who went around spying on people to find out if they'd had a nervous breakdown?

I don't remember anything at all of what happened in school that afternoon. All I could think about was having a nervous breakdown. I thought that people who did that must shake all over because your hands could shake when you got nervous. I wondered if my mother was in the hospital shaking all over. I even forgot about Rosie being sick, so on the way home I stopped in at Pearl's house to pick her up. Pearl's mother told me didn't I remember? Mrs. Cavanaugh had gone to our house to take care of her.

I went on home, mad that I'd gone two blocks out of the way to pick up Rosie and mad that I had to go home every day after school to take care of her.

I walked slow and threw some stones just to see how far I could throw them. I couldn't throw them anywhere near far enough to cheer me up. I couldn't do anything right.

When I got home, Dr. Lomvick's car was parked in front of the house.

Dr. Lomvick was putting away his thermometer and stethoscope in his black case.

"No," he said, "it isn't scarlet fever."

He snapped the case shut and told Mrs. Cavanaugh to give Rosie part of an aspirin every so often and to sponge her with warmish water. It was about all he could say to do. Mrs. Cavanaugh told me she would stay overnight and sleep on the couch to look after her.

But her staying didn't help. Rosie was still sick in the morning. I told her good-bye before I went to school. I was glad it wasn't scarlet fever. I'd had that and that's why I had to wear such thick glasses. But I knew she felt awful. Her face was red, and her arm was so hot when I touched it, I didn't know what to say.

That made Thursday bad.

Mrs. Cavanaugh couldn't stay Thursday night, but she'd come back first thing in the morning. My father took care of Rosie that night.

Rosie whimpered a lot. Once, I woke up and heard her talking loud. She sounded strange, not really like Rosie. In the morning she didn't say anything. She just kept whimpering. I got to feel sick when I heard her and I wished she wouldn't.

Friday was awful.

That day at school when it came time for English, Miss Goodlatty said, "Class, Ritchie's little sister is very ill. I think it would be nice if we each wrote her a letter to say we hoped she would be better soon."

I wondered how she knew. *I* hadn't told her.

Everybody looked at me. Sue Kolinsky made a kind of sad face. Greg Wojnak curled up his top lip. I could just hear him thinking, *Gluck!* I wondered if I had to write a letter too. Miss Goodlatty said I did.

Then she asked me, "Ritchie, is there anything Rosie especially likes? Maybe we can tell her something to cheer her up."

I couldn't think of anything at first. Then I said, "She likes the story of the Three Billy Goats Gruff. She likes to pretend the troll lives under the bridge that goes over the creek."

Everybody laughed and I felt stupid. I was mad at myself for telling on Rosie. I thought the whole idea of writing letters to her was stupid because Rosie couldn't read yet.

After school I had twenty-six pieces of paper to carry home to Rosie. When we were outside, Melvin Collins made a face at me and talked high through his nose. "Ritchie's little sister's sick! Let's write her a letter." Then his voice got like it always was. "Be sure to read her mine, goggles. It'll really make her feel good. The big one will make you feel good too. You just wait and see."

He said "the big one" as if it had a line drawn under it. He hadn't forgotten. All at once I wished he'd do it, whatever it was. I wished he'd do it and get it over with.

I walked home slow. Miss Goodlatty had told me I should read the letters to Rosie. I started looking at them while I walked. Most of them said, "Dear Rosie, I hope you feel better soon." And then something like: we played hopscotch today, or marbles, or read about the United States, or did lots of long division, and then, Sincerely yours, and signed their names. One letter wasn't signed. It said, "to bad yor mother is crazy." I knew that was Melvin Collins's letter. He always left the *u* out of "your." I tore it up and felt worse than I'd ever felt in my life. Was having a nervous breakdown being crazy?

And then I even felt worse than that, because there by the side of the road on the edge of the field near our house was Thad Grailowsky's dog, Blackie. He'd been hit by a car. He was dead.

Four

I stood there with the letters in my hand and stared at poor old Blackie. What should I do? Dead dogs got picked up after a while by the city. There were a lot of stray dogs around. People couldn't afford to feed them and they'd turn them loose at the edge of town. You'd see them, skinny and frightened, and sometimes somebody would call the dog pound and the dog catcher would come around and pick them up. Sometimes there would even be packs of dogs running loose. You had to be careful. But this was Blackie. He wasn't a stray.

I looked at old Blackie and I thought, The city will pick him up. Then I thought, Thad Grailowsky'll be looking for him. I thought of the nice look in Thad Grailowsky's eyes that time on the trolley, and I thought, I don't care what he has to do with Chicago.

So I started across the field to his shack. All at once I remembered how a long time ago there used to be a path between his shack and our house when he brought tomatoes to us. That was so long ago, I never even remembered it until now!

After all this time the path was gone.

I was scared when I got to his door and didn't knock very loud. I thought he must have the radio on because I could hear music. Sunday afternoons my mother listened to the New York Philharmonic on the radio. She'd bring Rosie in and make me come down to listen too. I'd lie on the floor and read the Sunday funnies while the music went on. Sometimes it was really special and I'd forget the funnies and listen.

It wasn't a whole orchestra coming out of Thad Grailowsky's shack, just one instrument—I thought it might be a cello—playing classical music. Not many of the kids at school heard classical music, so I never told them I liked it. Hearing it coming now gave me a lonely feeling that was sad and good at the same time. Like having our mother there a little bit.

I didn't want to knock again, and I started to turn around to go home, but then I thought about old Blackie, and knocked again. This time the music stopped and in a minute Thad Grailowsky opened the door. He stood looking at me, surprised and maybe wondering who I was.

"Your dog got hit by a car," I said. "He's dead by the road." I pointed back across the field.

"Oh," he said. "Oh. I was wondering where he was." His voice surprised me. It sounded just like I knew it would. He was still a minute, and then he said, "Blackie? You're sure?" I nodded. "Oh," he said, and looked away a minute. Then he cleared his throat. "Well . . . well, I'll go and get him. Thanks for telling me, Ritchie."

He did know who I was.

I could have gone home then, but I didn't. I didn't want to. I don't know what I wanted to do. I just didn't want to go home and hear Rosie crying. I stood there looking at him, and then I said, "Can I help you?"

He kept looking at me as if he was thinking. Then he said, "Sure. I guess you can, Ritchie. We'll get an old blanket and the wheelbarrow. We'll bury him. You can help me."

Then he noticed I had all those papers in my hand.

"You better put those down. Here, come on in and put them there on the table." When he said "down," the *d* had a kind of fat *dh* sound.

I'd never been in his shack before. I thought it would be like old man Bosley's shack that I was in once when my mother made me take him a jar of soup. Old man Bosley's shack was three little dark cramped rooms full of stuff— old clothes, cigar butts in jars, old boots and a rusty snow shovel and newspapers stacked in the corners. The kitchen part had a greasy black stove and the sink was full of dirty dishes and pans.

But Thad Grailowsky's shack wasn't like that. There was one big room with the kitchen part on one side with a narrow table between it and the rest of the room. The other part of the room had a couch and two more chairs and a desk and a piano. A violincello leaned on a kitchen chair with a music stand in front of it. On one wall a wide bookcase filled with books went right to the ceiling. On another wall there was a really nice picture of a boat and some men on a beach. There was a door to another room. The windows were small, but the sun came in in such a nice way it made it all seem warm and friendly and it was as clean as our house. I guess people called it a shack because it probably only had two rooms and the outside needed paint.

I put the papers down on the table beside a plate of tomatoes.

"It's the last of them," Thad Grailowsky said when he saw me looking at the tomatoes. "I just picked them. It's supposed to freeze tonight."

"They sure used to be good," I said. It was funny how I remembered the tomato taste all of a sudden—like remembering the path.

"Have one," he said, and I did while he went to look for an old blanket. The tomato was still warm from the sun. I licked the side of my hand where the juice ran down and wiped my chin on my sleeve.

I wheeled the wheelbarrow for him to where the dog was. He covered Blackie up and wrapped the blanket under him and put him in the barrow. He wheeled it back and then wondered where to bury him.

"He liked to lie in the front yard," I said.

He nodded. "That was his favorite place," he said. So we decided the place to bury him was the special place he liked.

He got a shovel and started to dig there. I knew Thad Grailowsky felt bad, so I felt bad too, but I didn't know what to say.

"How's everybody at your house?" he asked while he dug.

I said, "Okay." And then I said, "Well, not really. Rosie is sick with a fever." And then, I don't know why, I said, "Our mother is in the hospital."

"I know," he said.

That surprised me because I never saw him talking to anybody. He certainly didn't talk to my father, so how would he know? Then I thought, here was somebody who lived just the block behind us my whole life who was burying his dead dog I'd told him about who knew about me and I didn't know anything about him except what other people said. Mostly Aunt Vickie. I thought about all the books in his house and thought he must know a lot. All of a sudden I had to ask something because somehow I thought he wouldn't laugh like Melvin Collins would. Somehow I thought he wouldn't say nothing, like my father would. Somehow I thought he would tell me. So I asked.

"What's a nervous breakdown, Mr. Grailowsky?"

But he didn't answer me. He stared down in the hole for a minute, and then he said, "I guess it's deep enough."

I was disappointed and felt ashamed, like I shouldn't have asked.

We put old Blackie, all wrapped in the blanket, in the hole and I helped shovel the dirt in over him. We washed the dirt off our hands under the outside faucet.

Then he said, "Come on in and have some bread and a glass of milk."

I decided he'd forgotten about what I asked him. The

bread and milk sounded good and I wanted to see the inside of his house again, so I said okay.

We washed our hands with soap at the kitchen sink. He cut some bread—it wasn't already sliced—and put butter and peanut butter on it. Then he put sliced tomatoes and a little salt on top and some leaf lettuce on top of that and then another slice of bread and butter. He put it all on a plate. He didn't make another sandwich. He poured out a glass of milk for me and one for him and pushed the plate toward me. We sat at the table with the letters from the kids at school.

That was the best sandwich I ever had. While I was eating it, he said, "I don't know much about nervous breakdowns. There are all kinds of people in the world. I think they happen to different people for different reasons."

I drank some milk and went back to my sandwich again.

"Sometimes people get so tired they can't go on working and just have to go to bed and stay there," he said.

I knew my mother was busy all day, but I never thought she ever got that tired. Except sometimes she was too tired to play the piano. But then, my father never wanted her to play it anyway.

"There are probably other reasons too," Thad Grailowsky said after he had a drink of milk. "Sometimes they get lonely and start crying and can't stop. Sometimes there's something they want to do and they can never find time to do it. Sometimes they worry about everything. They forget about the good things and think about all the sad things there are in the world and just can't stand it. They get upset because they can't do anything about it."

I wondered if my mother was in bed, lonesome and crying and wanting to do something she couldn't do and being upset about the whole world. I couldn't imagine that. Except for lately, it always seemed to me she was happy because she could say funny things and laugh and blow into Rosie's neck and make Rosie laugh. She used to do it to me and I laughed too, until my father told her to stop.

"Do they ever get better?" I asked.

"Lots of times they do, after they've had enough rest and if people are nice to them."

I finished my sandwich and picked up the crumbs and ate them.

"Do you want another sandwich?" Thad Grailowsky asked.

"No." I shook my head.

"Have you visited your mother in the hospital?" he asked.

"No." I shook my head again. "My father said no."

"Does he go to see her?"

"Sometimes, I guess. Once anyway." But I wasn't sure.

He didn't say anything. We finished our milk and he poured out some more for me.

"What's wrong with Rosie?" he asked.

"She's got a fever," I said. "It won't go away. Mrs. Cavanaugh stays whenever she can. I better get home. I promised Rosie I'd read her 'The Three Billy Goats Gruff' today. It's her favorite story. Our mother used to read it to her. I read it to her yesterday too. She thinks the troll lives under the bridge by your house." Oh, no! I'd said it again, like I had to say it every time I opened my mouth.

But Thad Grailowsky didn't laugh. He said, "Little kids like to pretend. They have big imaginations. Too bad grown-up people lose theirs."

"Yeah," I said. "I guess I'm grown up because I told her he didn't live there." I stood up. "Too bad about Blackie."

"He was a good dog. He was old."

"Will you get another dog?"

"I don't know," he said.

"I always wanted a dog," I said, and then I felt ashamed, as if I was picking on my father for not letting me have a dog.

"Sometimes it doesn't work out," Thad Grailowsky said.

I nodded and went to the door.

"Don't forget your papers," he said.

"They're letters for Rosie from all the kids in the fifth grade," I told him while he handed them to me. "The teacher thought she might like to have them."

"That was nice," Thad Grailowsky said.

I'd never thought of Miss Goodlatty being nice. I thought she just wanted to make us practice heading up letters with the date and the return address and saying "Sincerely yours" the right way.

"Rosie can't read," I said. "She's supposed to start kindergarten after New Year's. Well, thanks for the sandwich, Mr. Grailowsky. Good-bye."

"Good-bye, Ritchie. Thanks for helping bury Blackie.

Drop in again for a talk. Let me know how you're doing. Let me know how Rosie is doing."

"Sure." I noticed the *dh* sound again. "Sure. Thanks again."

I went home through the field where I thought the old path used to be. I ran really fast, not because I knew Mrs. Cavanaugh would be mad that I was late, but because I wanted to cry. It was an awful feeling because I was too old for that. Why should I want to cry? Was it because old Blackie was dead? What did I care about old Blackie? I hadn't felt like crying when we buried him, just kind of sad for Thad Grailowsky. I hadn't felt like crying until Thad Grailowsky said, "Drop in again for a talk. Let me know how you're doing."

I didn't cry though—not then.

Mrs. Cavanaugh did scold me. She was sitting in the front room with her coat and hat on and holding her big old black pocketbook on her lap. She scolded me all the while she got up and went to the door, but it didn't last long because she had to catch the trolley. I didn't cry then, either.

After she left, I went up to see Rosie. She was lying there looking at the ceiling. When she saw me come in, she looked at me.

"I want Mama," she said, and started to cry. All of a sudden I started to cry. "I do too," I said, and then I stopped crying fast because boys don't cry.

But Rosie'd seen me cry and she looked at me. I looked at her, and we knew—we just knew—that we both wanted her and that we hadn't said anything about it before because we couldn't, but now we could. I put my face down next to hers, not hard because I knew she hurt all over from the fever. She put her arms around my neck.

"Get better, Rosie," I whispered. "Get better fast."

She hugged me a little. She was hot, but somehow I was sure she'd be better tomorrow.

After that I told her about the letters and sat down beside her and read them to her. All except Melvin Collins's that I'd torn up. I didn't tell her about Thad Grailowsky, either, because I didn't want to tell her Blackie was dead. I read "The Three Billy Goats Gruff" to her until we heard my father come in the door downstairs.

Five

I warmed up the canned peas and took the macaroni and cheese out of the oven and put it on the kitchen table. My father and I always ate in the kitchen.

"Miss Goodlatty had everybody write a letter to Rosie today," I said.

"Oh?" my father said.

"She thought it would cheer her up."

"Um."

"Mr. Grailowsky's dog got hit by a car."

My father didn't say anything, so I didn't say any more either. But for the first time in my life I was mad because my father didn't like to be bothered when he was eating. I washed the dishes while he went upstairs to go to the bathroom and to check on Rosie.

"Is she okay?" I asked when he came down.

"She's asleep," he said.

"That's good," I said. "Do you think she'll sleep all night?"

My father didn't say anything. He didn't look at me. He went into the other room.

I went upstairs after I'd wiped the dishes. Rosie was still asleep, so I came back downstairs. Miss Goodlatty had told me to do some extra long division for homework. I sat at the dining-room table and did all the problems. I wondered why they seemed easy tonight. Long division really wasn't that hard. After that I listened to *The Lone Ranger*. I kept the radio soft with my ear against it so it wouldn't bother my father while he read the newspaper. Then I went to my room and looked for something I hadn't read. But there were only my own books that I'd already read. I wished I had *The Count of Monte Cristo*. I'd have to find some way to get it back. We were supposed to give a book report at the end of next week.

I took *Wild Animals I Have Known* out of my bookcase. I'd read it twice before, but I'd never done a book report on it. Miss Goodlatty wouldn't know the difference. I started looking through it to remind me of some of the stories, and then I started thinking about what Thad Grailowsky had said.

I wondered if our mother got tired. When she did things, she always made Rosie and me laugh. When she scrubbed the floors, she'd say whoever walked on the wet linoleum would get fed to Thad Grailowsky's chickens. When she washed fingerprints off the walls, she'd say next time she caught the burglars who put them there, she'd make them eat leftover parsnips on their cornflakes. When she cleaned the closets and cupboards and put fresh papers in the drawers, she'd say she was looking for a baseball bat to swat flies with. When she was darning stockings or sewing on buttons, she would growl and look fierce when she bit off the thread. It always seemed like she was having as much fun as we were. I didn't know if she was. I started to read.

After a while my father came up the stairs. He told me to turn off the light.

Saturday morning Rosie was a little better, the way I thought she'd be, but Sunday she was worse again. Then on Monday Mrs. Cavanaugh said her fever wasn't as high, and maybe she wouldn't have to go to the hospital after all.

I wished Thad Grailowsky's house was the other way from us so that I could take a shortcut through the field to school every day and stop and tell him how Rosie was. Tuesday I decided to drop in after school. He'd told me to, hadn't he? Just for a few minutes. I'd let him know how Rosie was.

I went the long way around and knocked on the door, but he wasn't home. It made me feel like he didn't want to see me. I was so disappointed, I didn't try again until Friday.

This time he was home.

"Hello, Ritchie!" he said, and opened the door wide. "I was wondering why you didn't come for a visit."

"I've been busy," I said, and felt better again.

We talked a while. I told him school wasn't so bad. I told him Rosie was a little better today.

"Sue Kolinsky told Miss Goodlatty that for an assignment somebody should write Rosie a letter every week," I told him.

Miss Goodlatty thought that was a good idea, so every Friday somebody had to write a letter to Rosie. Sue Kolinsky had to do it today because it was her idea.

"Nobody wants to," I said. "I don't either, but they all hate me for it. Melvin Collins is really mad. He said he'd get me for it. He should get Sue Kolinsky! It wasn't my idea!"

"He can't pick on a girl," Thad Grailowsky said.

"He does, though," I said. "He waits until no grown-ups are around and then he twists a girl's arm if he's mad at her. He picks on boys, too, when they're smaller than he is."

"Is he bigger than you?"

"Yeah."

"Are you afraid of him?"

"I don't know." I shrugged and looked down. "He's tough."

Melvin Collins had pushed me down some more. He was always getting even for something, I never knew what. But none of those were "the big one." He'd reminded me of it every time he pushed me down.

"Anyway, if he writes a letter, I'll tear it up. He can't spell," I said.

Thad Grailowsky laughed. "I never could spell either," he said. "And I don't like to write letters. I'd rather play music." Then he showed me how he played his cello and we talked about his piano—how his upright was different from our grand piano.

"My mother could play the piano," I told him.

"I know." Thad Grailowsky nodded his head.

That surprised me again. How did he know all these things?

"She was giving me lessons," I said.

"Can you play something for me?" Thad Grailowsky asked.

"No. I haven't practiced since she got sick. I used to practice before school in the morning after my father went to the office. But now he waits until Mrs. Cavanaugh comes. By then it's time for me to go to school."

"Can't you practice while your father is waiting? You should play some pieces every day," Thad Grailowsky said.

"My father doesn't like to hear me practice. He didn't like to hear our mother play."

"Do it before he gets home at night."

I hadn't thought of doing it at all. Maybe I would when I got home.

I went home through the field. I thought about how in the summer the grass was tall and green and full of blue grassflowers and buttercups and dandelions. There were meadowlark nests and garter snakes and wild rabbits. The grass was brown now because of the frosts. Tonight it was supposed to rain. It might even snow.

I did want to play the piano when I got home, but Rosie wanted me to read to her, so I read Sue Kolinsky's letter. It said:

> Dear Rosie,
>   I hope you are feeling better. We are doing
> lots of long divishion. I am reading The Wizard

of Oz. It is about a girl named Dorothy. She
has a dog named Toto. They meet the
Munchkins and a Scarcrow.

> *Sincerely yours,*
> *Sue Kolinsky*

I was kind of disappointed. I thought maybe Sue Kolinsky would write something about the Billy Goats Gruff.

But it was all right anyway. The letter was something to give to Rosie, and it was a lot longer than the first time. Besides, our mother had read *The Wizard of Oz* to Rosie last year. I read the letter twice, and afterward we talked about the Cowardly Lion and remembered some of the rest of the book while Rosie ate some cornflakes and milk.

Then I took her to the bathroom. I'd walk with her to the bathroom door and wait for her to come out. I remembered when I had a fever how cold the toilet seat was.

"Are you okay?" I asked, and piggybacked her to bed. Sometimes I piggybacked her both ways. She was awful light and skinny. She never wanted to eat anything and a lot of times she threw up when she did.

When she was back in bed, she wanted me to read "The Three Billy Goats Gruff" to her, but there wasn't time because my father came home. At supper I told him that somebody was going to write a letter to Rosie once a week.

"Um," he said.

I gave up saying anything else.

It rained all weekend.

40

On Monday when I got home from school, there was a surprise. When I took the mail out of the box, there was a real letter with a three-cent stamp on it. For Rosie. I noticed it because it was on the top of the bills and things. It was in printing: MISS ROSEMARY WILLIS, and our address. There was no return address. Just the letters T.U.B. in the top left-hand corner. I turned it over. There was no return address on the back, either.

I wanted to open it so bad to see who it was from that I almost did, but I knew Rosie would want to open it even more. She'd never gotten a letter in the mailbox with a real three-cent stamp on it. And she didn't have anything to do but lie in bed and look at old picture books or stare at the ceiling or through the window at the sky. If she felt really good, she sat up and cut out paper dolls. Sometimes she pretended to read "The Three Billy Goats Gruff." She knew just when to turn the pages because she knew it by heart.

"I'm home," I called to Mrs. Cavanaugh, and ran upstairs with Rosie's letter.

Rosie was propped up on her pillows. That meant she was feeling a little better.

"Look here!" I said, and put the letter in front of her. "It's for you!"

Rosie stared at it. Her eyes were big around.

"How do you know?" she asked.

"It says your name on it. There! 'Rosemary Willis.' "

"Is that what it says?"

"You know your letters! See there! *R* for Rosemary."

"Everybody calls me Rosie."

"It's still *R*," I told her. "It's still for you. Open it up. See who it's from."

She didn't want to tear the envelope.

"Ritchie?" Mrs. Cavanaugh called up the stairs. "I'm going now. There's stew on the stove keeping warm. Don't let it burn. Good-bye!"

"Thanks, Mrs. Cavanaugh. Good-bye!" I heard the door open and close. "Here's my jackknife. You can slice it open." I pulled up the blade and showed her how to slip it in the end of the envelope under the flap. "It'll open easy that way."

She did it, but the knife slipped and tore the envelope down a ways. She almost cried when it did that.

"Never mind," I told her. "Envelopes always do that. Let's see what the letter says."

She pulled it out and opened it up. There were two pages on both sides, and the printing was pretty small. It was a long letter.

At the top was the return address. I read the top line: "porolli doumuob illoroq, troll."

My eyes stayed on that last word.

"Troll?" Rosie asked, her eyes opening wider.

I nodded.

"What else?" she asked.

I read:

> *"porolli doumuob illoroq, troll*
> *third small hole on the left*
> *under the drondic bridge, PLTR*
> *nosqualtic 38, 9132"*

"What's that?" Rosie asked.

"I don't know! It's whoever wrote it," I said, and kept staring at the first line: *porolli doumuob illoroq, troll.* "Like on Sue Kolinsky's letter. Her name and where she lives and the day it is."

She had Sue Kolinsky's letter on the bed. I guess Mrs. Cavanaugh had read it to her. Mrs. Cavanaugh was nice that way. I showed Rosie.

"Read some more," Rosie said.

I looked at "troll" once more and then read, "Dear rosenander."

"That's not me. That's somebody else!" The corners of Rosie's mouth turned down. Her eyes got full of tears.

"Keep still," I said. "It's got your name on the envelope. It has to be for you. Listen!"

Six

D*ear rosenander,*

*I am calling you rosenander instead of Rosie
or Rosemary because I am a troll and
rosenander is the only name we have for what
you are named after, which is rosemary. I have
rosenander in my garden. It is a bush with
little thin dark green leaves and blue flowers
and tastes awfully good on bidlicks, which are
something like your tiny new potatoes. If you
are named Rose and Mary, that is different,
but I think of you as rosenander, so I hope you
don't mind my calling you that.*

I looked at Rosie. Her eyes were so big they took up
almost all her face—except her mouth, which was hanging open.

"See? It's for you all right," I said, and then read some
more:

*You are probably wondering why I am
writing to you. First of all it's because you
are the only person in the world who ever
knew that I live under the bridge behind
your house. That's the name of the bridge on
the letter: drondic bridge. But the mailman
doesn't know it. If you wrote to me, he
would never know where to take your letter.
He wouldn't be able to find my mailbox,
either. (It is the third small hole on the
left.) If he was really smart, and knew this
was the drondic bridge, he would leave your
letter under the big rock on the low end of
the bridge with a corner of the paper sticking
out so I could see it, but I don't think he
knows.*

*I am also writing to you to let you know that
I won't eat you if you cross my bridge, even if
you would taste good with bidlicks. I won't eat
your brother, either, because I am not a big
mean troll. I am small and insignificant.
Besides, other than an occasional fish, I am
really a vegetarian.*

It took me a while to figure out "insignificant," but I
finally sounded it out and told Rosie, "I think it means the
troll doesn't amount to much."

"What's a vetegearian?" she asked.

"Vegetarian," I said. "Somebody who lives on peas and
lettuce."

"Read some more," she said.

So I read some more:

> The main reason I am writing to you is this: All of my brothers got big, the way trolls should, and went off to make trouble along with the other big trolls who live under the railroad bridges. Big trolls live under railroad bridges because they love to shout and yell and bang things around. When the trains go over, they can make all the noise they want to and no one hears them. They have a lot of fun. But I don't. I'm all alone. None of them ever comes to visit me. I think they've forgotten I'm here. Mother and Father don't come either. They are busy taking care of my grandmother and grandfather who are taking care of my great-g. and -g. who are taking care of my great-great-g. and -g. (g. and g. stand for "grandmother" and "grandfather"—this way I don't have to write it out each time.) Every one of them is too old to come to visit me, and the thing is, I'm lonesome.
>
> To make matters worse, something bad came along and I'm frightened half to death. Since you are the only person from up there who knows I'm here, I'm hoping you can help me. Don't worry, you won't have to fight this bad thing. For one thing, you can't, because you are a very little girl and you're not feeling

well. All I want you to do is be my friend, even if you can't see me. That will help me more than anything in the world. Will you?

Oh dear, I wanted to say more, but I have almost run out of paper. I shall write again as soon as I can sneak into Kulich's corner store just before he closes. Then I will find the paper and slide it under the crack beneath the door, one sheet at a time. I will leave rare-green-flat-round creek pebbles on the counter to pay for it. Then I will tiptoe into the back part of the store where he lives and hide behind the ice box until Mrs. Kulich takes out the garbage. Then I will hide in her shadow and follow her outside. (She never looks behind her when she is taking out the garbage.) Then I'll go around to the front door and pick up the paper and run home as fast as I can. I hope it doesn't rain and spoil the paper.

Yours faithfully and honestly,
porolli doumuob illoroq, troll

p.s. You may call me pod.

p.p.s. Sometimes it takes a long time to get paper that way. Then it takes me a long time to write a letter because I have to write it big enough so you can read it. It might be days and days before you hear from me, but I promise I will write. Don't lose hope.

pod

I sat there staring at the letter.

Rosie said, "Read it again."

I read it again.

"Read it again," she said.

I read it again.

Then she said, "It's for me. From a real live troll! A *good* troll! He wants me to be his friend!"

"Rosie," I started to say. "Rosie, there aren't . . ." But I couldn't go on and say ". . . any trolls." Because . . . because . . . well, she was so excited. And besides, who *did* write this letter? I turned the pages over and turned them back. Even if Sue Kolinsky was the smartest girl in the class, I didn't think she could have written it. It was too long. Besides, how would she have known how to spell his fancy name and the return address with "nosqualtic" in it?

"Where's his name? Where's 'pod'?" Rosie was asking.

I pointed to "pod" at the bottom of the second page.

"P-O-D," she read. "That's 'pod'?"

"How can you read it upside down?" I asked, because I was holding the paper my way.

"It isn't upside down," she said. "It says P-O-D right there." She pointed.

I turned the paper over. Sure enough. It said "pod" upside down and right side up.

For some reason that made me feel strange. As if there was some kind of magic in it.

"Isn't that something?" I whispered.

Seven

The stew hadn't burned. Not black, anyway. Rosie was so excited, she ate her whole supper and didn't throw up. I read the letter to her again before she went to sleep. I read it to her the next morning while she ate her poached egg on toast. I was almost late for school.

I read that letter to Rosie when I got home from school. She had it under her pillow. I asked her if Mrs. Cavanaugh had read it to her.

"No," she said. "Nobody else can know. You're the only one."

She didn't show it to my father, either. I think she was afraid he'd leave some words out, because he'd read "The Three Billy Goats Gruff" to her once and he left out some of the words. He wouldn't put them back when she asked him to, so she didn't ask him to read to her anymore.

I was glad she didn't show him the letter. I knew he thought make-believe stories were silly, that grown-up people shouldn't have anything to do with pretend or magic or wizards—anything like that. But our mother liked them, and Rosie loved them. I liked them too, though sometimes I felt funny about it. I wondered if it was all right for girls to like them, but that boys shouldn't, that my father really meant boys when he said grown-ups. Even so, once I started reading one, I forgot about whether I should like it or not. If it was good, I just kept reading it. I'd think about it afterward, and wonder if maybe ... I mean, what if there *was* magic?

I read the letter to her after school and before school every day.

"I hide it in my drawer until Mrs. Cavanaugh is through fluffing up my pillow," she told me. "Then I take it out and put it where my hand can hold it."

The letter was getting more wrinkled up all the time.

On Thursday she asked when I thought another letter might come.

"I don't know," I told her. "Pod said it might be days and days, and it's only been three days now."

"What day did it come on?" she wanted to know.

"Monday," I told her. "Today's Thursday. Monday, Tuesday, Wednesday, Thursday."

"Then what?" she asked.

"Friday, Saturday, Sunday. Then Monday again."

"Do you think another one will come on Monday?"

"How should I know? Don't be a pest," I told her.

On Friday I brought home a letter from Charlie Allen. We were writing letters according to our last names in the alphabet. Charlie Allen, Angeline Belondo, Melvin Collins. That was fine with me. Ritchie Willis would be almost the last one. Weeks and weeks away. Rosie would be in school by then and I wouldn't have to write one. Neither would Eddy Yordy.

Of course I kept wondering if another letter with a three-cent stamp on it would really come from—whoever wrote it. I looked through the mail every day, but there was nothing there for Rosie.

I took Charlie Allen's letter to her after I stopped in to say hello to Thad Grailowsky. He was feeding a skinny little short-haired dog—white with black spots.

"A stray," he said.

We watched it wolf down the dog food and then throw up.

"I gave it too much," Thad Grailowsky said while he cleaned up the floor. He warmed a little milk and tore a piece of bread into it for the dog. The dog ate it just as fast, only this time it didn't throw up. It kept watching Thad Grailowsky. It wanted more.

"I'll give it a little more in half an hour," he said.

I felt sorry for the dog—that it had to wait another half an hour. I went across the field thinking how Thad Grailowsky hadn't yelled and thrown the dog out the door when it threw up. He hadn't even looked mad like my father did when Rosie threw up. He'd just gone ahead and cleaned up the mess as if cleaning up dog messes was just an ordinary thing anybody had to do.

I don't know why that made me feel good.

When I got home, I read Charlie Allen's letter to Rosie.

Dear Rosie,

I hope you are better soon. You should see how far I hit the ball yesterday. It was a home run.

Sincerely,
Charlie Allen

"Did he?" Rosie asked.

"Yeah," I said.

Then I read pod's letter. We decided to keep his letter under the paper in the drawer with Rosie's underwear all day every day so it didn't get wrinkled anymore. Rosie could take it out if she had to.

It rained again Saturday and Sunday. Mrs. Cavanaugh didn't come on the weekends. My father got up and shoveled coal into the furnace in the basement. After breakfast he did the grocery shopping. I hoped he would bring home something besides sausage and macaroni, but he didn't. He came home and put stuff away and listened to the radio and took a nap and read the newspaper and did the crossword puzzle and studied some chess problems. He said not to bother him.

It was a boring weekend. I read to Rosie and I read to myself. On Sunday afternoon Aunt Vickie brought Rosie some new paper dolls. There were lots of them—the Dionne quintuplets. Aunt Vickie talked loud to my father about how hard something must be for him to cope with. I heard her go on and on, but I didn't listen to what she said.

I worked on my model airplane. I was really careful with the razor blade. I didn't want the balsa wood to split or get a chunk carved out of it while I cut out the parts. I hoped the plane would fly when it was finished. I knotted the rubber bands together and stretched them and twisted them. They were strong. One of these days they would hook into the inside of the frame of the Piper Cub. Then I'd cover it with thin paper and I'd take it out into the field and wind the propeller around and around and off it would go!

Sunday night Rosie had her paper dolls lined up on the bed. She knew all their names. "Marie, Annette, Cecile, Emily, and Yvonne," she told me. "Read all the letters to them—Sue Kolinsky's, Charlie Allen's, and pod's."

After pod's, Rosie started worrying about the rain.

"What if pod didn't get to the store until today?" she said. "What if the paper got all wet?"

"The store isn't open on Sunday," I told her. But I couldn't help wondering myself.

It was still raining Monday morning. Rosie didn't want to eat any cornflakes, but I said she had to. What would pod think if she didn't? For the first time I wondered what she did all day long with Mrs. Cavanaugh there. She couldn't get out of bed more than a few minutes at a time. Talk about boring!

School was boring too that day. I kept looking at the clock. I kept wondering if there would be a letter for Rosie in the mailbox. She would be pretty disappointed if there wasn't one.

But there was. I saw the T.U.B. right away.

"Hey, Rosie!" I shouted, and threw down my jacket and ran up the stairs.

This time she was very careful about the way she slit open the envelope. She didn't tear it at all.

The letter started just like before, first with the same return address, except the numbers. It said "nosqualtic 45, 9132." I wondered what "nosqualtic" with the numbers was. Then:

Dear rosenander,

You have no idea what a hard time I had getting this paper. But first I have to tell you about the Gornuck, because it was all the Gornuck's fault that getting the paper was hard.

But before that, I have to make you promise not to be frightened, because if you are going to be frightened, Ritchie can't read you the rest of this letter. And I'll tell you why.

On my honor as an insignificant troll, I have to be honest. And being honest means I have to say there are lots of things in the world that are lovely, but there are some things that are sad and some things that are bad and some things that are frightening. If you are going to be too sad or too frightened, I don't want to tell you about them.

(You will have to tell Ritchie if you are, and

*he will not read the rest of this letter unless
you aren't. Okay?)*

My lips prickled and Rosie's eyes got absolutely huge,
but of course she said she was brave enough. I swallowed
and kept reading.

Eight

This is about the Gornuck, a nasty slimy creature that lives in the woods upstream from me. It looks at you as if it were thinking of all the ways it could make you miserable.

When I first came here to live under the bridge (that was after Mother and Father went to live with all the g. and g.'s, something just over two thousand years ago), the Gornuck was the first creature I met. I knew immediately that it was a krinkaw. (That's the kind of person you don't like very well.) Still, I was feeling very much alone, so even if I didn't like its looks, I decided to make friends with it. I invited it to dinner.

Dinner was at nine at night because the Gornuck only comes out then. I had done my best with small tangy chovits for appetizers,

grilled sandaviis (I ate more fish in those
days), braised hennaquas, bidlicks browned in
butter with garlic and rosenander, and for
dessert wild squimsquas tarts. All extremely
tasty, and not a girl, boy, or billy goat in the
lot.

The Gornuck came early, oozed himself into
my best chair, and snorted up all the chovits
while I was grilling the sandaviis. When it was
time to sit down to dinner, he ate with his
elbows on the table and his face in his plate.
He never more than grunted now and then
when I passed him another dish or politely
urged him on to fourths, which he took,
licking the bowl besides with his long slimy
tongue, which he rolled up in the underside of
his mouth each time he finished licking a
dish.

"Licked the dishes with a *slimy* tongue?" Rosie asked.
"That's what it says," I told her.
"Uggy! What else?"
". . . finished licking a dish."
"You already said that," Rosie said.
"Keep still. I was just finding the place," I told her.

. . . finished licking a dish. (I had a dreadful
time washing the slime off the plates when I
did the dishes.) He looked at me only once—a
sidewise glance, cold and shifty. After the
cli'hom (a kind of drink only trolls know how

*to brew) and squimsquas tart (all of which he
ate—I had been hoping for a piece left over
for breakfast the next morning), he belched
prodigiously—*

"What's 'belched projidusly'?" Rosie asked.
"Burped," I said. I wasn't sure about the other word.
Rosie giggled. She hadn't giggled for a long time. I kept
reading.

> *. . . rolled himself out of the chair, and said,
> "Gotta go now. I got things to do at home."*
>
> *He didn't say "Thank you." He didn't say
> "Good-bye." He didn't offer to help pick up
> the dishes. He simply schloozed out the door,
> creezed down the riverbank, and plopped into
> the shallows. I could hear him slogging and
> sploshing his way upstream.*
>
> *I never had a thank-you note, I never had a
> return invitation. I never had such an
> ungrateful guest. I never invited him again. In
> fact, I avoided his part of the woods after I saw
> him lying on the big flat gray-and-purple rock
> that used to stick up out of the water. He was
> sprawled out, catching frogs the way frogs
> catch mosquitoes. You know, one long swoop
> of the three-foot-long tongue and a creature
> vanished. Bullfrogs, rabbits, and . . . ugh! I
> shudder at the memory! But he thrived on his
> diet and grew.*
>
> *Well, that was a long, long time ago. I didn't*

see him for five hundred years. About a hundred and fifty years ago, I decided he was gone for good, and I was glad.

I've lived in peace here under the drondic bridge with an occasional fox or weasel for company. Sometimes a young rabbit will sleep on my feet during the winter—warm and furry. I've gardened on the bank, fished from the river for eons, and made do, even the last seven years with that big black dog sniffing around my place.

Actually, the dog wasn't a krinkaw. He and I became friends. But now—oh dear, one of your dreadful bangbotters struck poor old Fangle and he is no more. I do wonder if Fangle and others like him weren't the reason I hadn't seen the Gornuck these past few years. Because last week, just after Fangle's demise, I heard it after more than six hundred years! The Gornuck! Sliming and sloshing in the creek just below my place under the bridge. There was no mistaking the sound of him. I shook from headhair to toeclaw.

Then, the very evening I was going out to Kulich's store for paper, I happened to look out the window and there he was, lying on the bluff on the other side of the creek and staring at the bank where my mailbox hole is. He had his usual greedy hungry look, but what was worse, he was huge. In that five hundred years,

I hadn't grown at all, but he was the size of a mammoth. (rosenander, Ritchie can explain what that is.)

I have no idea where he kept himself all this time. Has he come back to live at the bottom of the pool in the quarry below the brickyard now that no one is digging there anymore? It is such a deep pool! It's the only thing I can think of.

Worse, has he remembered that good dinner I gave him eons ago and come back looking for more? He is so big, I wonder if he has come looking for me.

I suppose you are wondering what this has to do with you. It has a great deal to do with you, and I hope you won't be frightened, but I will have to tell you later because, oh dear, I must stop and build some kind of wall against him in case you can't help me.

With great affection, and until the next letter,

       Your most honest troll, pod.

p.s. I looked for a letter under that rock, but there was none there. I would love a note— even a small slip of paper with just your name on it, or initials, if you can, so I know that my letters have come to you. I do hope the Gornuck didn't find and eat anything you may have sent.

p.p.s. Please don't show my letters to anyone

*else! I know you and Ritchie can, but most
people can't keep a secret, and if it gets out
that you are going to help me, who knows
what the Gornuck might do!"*

Of course I had to read the letter over and over to
Rosie. Her eyes were so big, you could hardly see the rest
of her face. I knew she'd been scared the first time
through by all the slimy stuff about the Gornuck. I had to
swallow to wet my mouth just because it got so dry from
reading aloud. By the end of the third time, she was more
excited than scared, but by the end of the fourth time, she
started being scared for pod. We both called him pod now,
and we talked a lot about what he might be doing.

"How can we help him?" she wondered.

"He'll have to tell us," I said.

"He can't wait all the way to next Monday to tell us," she
said. "He just can't do that or the Gornuck might eat him!"

"We still have to wait," I said. "Maybe tomorrow I can
go look under the bridge and see if he's started building a
wall."

"Take a letter to him. I want to make an *R* on a piece of
paper for him. Put it under the rock!" Rosie said.

I tore a piece of paper out of my school theme book and
brought her a pencil. She made a really good *R* for a not-
quite-five-year-old. Then I showed her how to make a *W*.
It was kind of wobbly, but she made it. Then she insisted
on doing "pod." She had to do it over a few times because
sometimes she got the *p* or the *d* backward. She crossed
them out until she got it right.

"You write the 'to' in front of it," she said. "I'm tired."

So I did, and folded the paper in half. "I'll put it under the rock in the morning," I told her. "That way the Gornuck won't be able to eat it. He only comes out at night."

Then we talked about where to keep pod's letters forever. My father never looked around for anything, so we didn't have to worry about him. There was Mrs. Cavanaugh and Aunt Vickie and our five cousins. They were pretty snoopy. We wanted to have some kind of secret place that nobody could get into, like a jewelry box with a key or something.

"I'll look in the dime store next Saturday," I told Rosie.

I had only thirty cents. I'd saved my allowance for three weeks toward another model airplane. That could wait. Even so, I knew it would take a long time to save up for a box like we wanted.

Meanwhile, the safest place was still under the paper lining in her middle drawer under her underwear. She wasn't using anything out of that drawer, so Mrs. Cavanaugh didn't have to open it to put anything away. Chances were Aunt Vickie wouldn't look there either. I slipped the two envelopes under the paper and straightened out her long brown stockings and put the vest with the garters on top of everything.

"Ritchie," Rosie called when I started to go out the door. I had to see about supper.

"Yeah?"

"Pod's mama went away too. So did his daddy and his brothers. You won't go away, will you?"

"Nah," I said, feeling kind of funny that she should ask. "Nah, I'll never go away."

Nine

I put the thermometer in Rosie's mouth before she had her cornflakes, and in a few minutes my father came in to read it.

"Um," he said.

"Is she better?" I asked.

He just shrugged, shook the thermometer, and went downstairs to wait for Mrs. Cavanaugh.

I kept hoping Rosie would be better, and some days she was. But today her cheeks were awfully pink.

"What about pod?" she asked after my father left the room. "What if the Gornuck ate him last night?"

"What if he didn't?" I said, though I'd been thinking that too. "Look, Rosie, pod has been there for years and years and the Gornuck didn't eat him. I don't think he can get into pod's house, and pod won't go out at night if he sees the Gornuck. He can take care of himself."

Even though she nodded, I could see that Rosie was

worried. Maybe that made her fever go up again. I gave her a soft hug good-bye.

On the way down the stairs I hoped she wouldn't worry all the way to next Monday when another letter might come. Then what if it didn't? What if the Gornuck *did* eat pod! Rosie might worry herself to death! I thought that because that was what people always said. Somebody was worried sick, or worried to death. But when I thought that, my stomach tightened up hard. Rosie was already sick, even if she had eaten more all last week and hadn't thrown up every day. What if she *did* worry herself to death? I mean, why would people say a thing like that if it never happened?

I thought about my mother having a nervous breakdown. Thad Grailowsky said some people worried themselves into one. Worried themselves sick! Oh, gosh! I felt terrible. Why had pod written those letters? Why didn't he tell us that nothing bad could happen to him?

"Oh, come on now," I said out loud. "Pod's all right."

"What did you say?" Mrs. Cavanaugh asked.

"Nothing," I said, and went out the door. I felt silly. I'd been talking as if pod was as real as Rosie thought he was! He couldn't be! But who wrote those letters?

I wondered about it all the way to school. It had to be somebody who knew Rosie liked "The Three Billy Goats Gruff," I figured, because of the troll living under the bridge. It could be anybody in my grade at school, because I'd told it to the whole class. But I didn't believe anybody in the class could write letters like that. Of course, Miss Goodlatty had heard. What if *she* had written them?

I shook my head. Somehow Miss Goodlatty didn't *seem* like the kind of person who would think of things like that. But how did I know? Maybe . . . Or who else? Did the teachers gossip and spy the way Aunt Vickie did? They'd all know, if they did. And Thad Grailowsky, I'd told him. And he'd known about my mother, so somebody told him things . . . but he was a grown-up man, and wouldn't make up a pretend troll. He'd said so himself. He'd said he couldn't spell, either, and all those big words were spelled right. Besides, he didn't like to write letters. But he could have told somebody else. And Mrs. Cavanaugh—*she* could have told somebody and they could have told . . . I mean, what if everybody in *town* knew that Rosie liked "The Three Billy Goats Gruff" and thought the troll lived under that bridge? It could be *anybody*!

But everybody didn't know Rosie. Why should somebody who didn't know some little kid scare her half to death by writing her a couple of letters?

"*Goofy* letters," I said out loud, and kicked a stone all the way across the street. Then I kicked another one even farther because I didn't really feel like those letters were goofy even if they were. I mean, it was more like reading a story, and I wanted to know what happened. Besides that, what if . . . what if . . . just what if pod *was* there? What if pod *had* written those letters?

I was glad to get to school and think about something else. I thought hard all day about everything that was going on—reading and spelling and arithmetic and art and recess and lunch. I even thought about how my bologna sandwich tasted and how the milk wasn't as cold as I like it. The whole thing all day long. Right up to the time for us to go home. All because I didn't want to think about Rosie worrying about pod from now until next Monday. By three thirty, when the bell rang, my brain was wiped out. I didn't even think about putting my glasses in the case until after I ran all the way home.

When I pulled the mail out of the top of the mailbox, my hands started shaking. I didn't expect there to be a letter because it was only Tuesday, but I could see there was a three-cent-stamp letter sticking up just a little at the top of the box. As fast as lightning, I thought it could be for my father. When my hands kept shaking, I wondered if I was having a nervous breakdown.

I pulled the letter out of the rest, and there, sure enough, was T.U.B. at the top of the envelope, and MISS ROSEMARY WILLIS and all the rest of it. The funniest feeling went all down my neck and arms right to my bottom, and then I shouted.

"Hey! Hey, Rosie!" and opened the door and slammed it and shouted, "Hey, Mrs. Cavanaugh! I'm home!" I threw the rest of the mail on the little table beside the door and ran up the stairs.

"Rosie, hey, Rosie," I said when I ran into her room. Then I stopped dead.

Rosie's room was all changed around. The little bookcase with the tall *Mother Goose* and *Aesop's Fables* books and the picture books in it was where her bed should be and the little desk and chair were against the other wall. Her bed was on the wrong side of the room, beside the window. The chest of drawers was on the other side of her bed. Rosie was sitting up with the pillows behind her. She was looking better.

"I asked Mrs. Cavanaugh to change me," she said. "Look, Ritchie, I can see Mr. Grailowsky's shack and a little bit of the bridge pod lives under. I've been watching to see if the Gornuck comes out."

I went to look through the window. It sure was just a *little* bit of the bridge, because it was way across the field. Almost a block away. All I could see was one post sticking up where the bridge crossed the creek. One post and where the path was and the trees and bushes and stuff that grew along the creek. Mostly you could see Thad Grailowsky's apple trees and garden and his shack.

"Hey, Rosie," I said. "That's swell. But look! It's only Tuesday, and here's another letter from pod!"

Ten

Dear rosenander,
   Yesterday was a purple-letter day for
me. First, I had a letter from you, and I thank
you so much for it. I am more grateful than
you can imagine. It is so nice to know that
someone nearby cares about you, even if they
can't see you!
   And it has made me feel so *brave*! Before I
felt so small and alone, but now I know I have
a friend! I almost feel as if I could go out and
smack that Gornuck right on the nose for
bothering me! Of course, I know I can't. I
can't even *reach* his nose! But it is a wonderful
feeling. Thank you. Thank you!
   Then I had a letter from *Father* after
hundreds of years! Think how I felt when I saw
the trollstamp from the hroustic bridge

MsLXA. (That's a Peruvian railroad bridge over a gorge in the Andes. Ritchie can tell you where the Andes are.) But was it bad news?

There was dread in my heart as I fetched my glasses and sat down at my desk by the window. By the way, I can see your window from here though you can't see mine because it is hidden by leaf shadows.

I think of you there now, not feeling well, and wonder if a little songdrip tea would cheer you up. I'd love to devise a way to slip some to you in in one of those bottles of milk the delivery man leaves, but perhaps I shouldn't. The milkman would fret if he thought someone was meddling with his bottles.

Well, to get on with Father's letter. It seems that not only Great-great-g. and -g., but Great-g. and -g., are becoming quite a handful.

(Now it's time to tell you a little more about me and our kind. Even though I am not a regular of our kind, it's not fair to ask you to help a total stranger. You need some family background.)

Troll history goes back into so long ago that I doubt you can imagine so many years. For instance, you count your years as one thousand nine hundred and thirty-nine, but as you see on my letter's date, I put nine thousand one hundred and thirty-two, and that's only since my great-great-g. and -g. were born. (Trolls count time from the birthday of their oldest living relatives. That's nosqualtic 1.) So Great-great-g. and -g. are nine thousand one hundred and thirty-two years and forty-six nosqualtic days old today.

Of course at such an age they have to have someone around to keep an eye on them, not because they fall or forget what they're doing, the way some old people do, but because the older they get, the more noise they make and the more trouble they cause.

This is because trolls began with the earth itself and were so used to all the upheavals—earthquakes, volcanoes, drenching rains, ferocious winds, blizzards, floods, fires, everything imaginable of an unsettling kind—that they came to think that that's the way things should be. So they love to create more disasters than there are now. That means one or two each week somewhere, for trolls have spread out all across the world. Java, Turkey, Norway—everywhere. (My close family happens to be mostly in South America.) So they do shake things up and blow things up, and the older they are, the better they get at doing it.

Young trolls (the usual kind—not like me) are just bad enough. They throw things and are noisy and obstreperous—general nuisances to you people. I should be doing all that too, but I've always been afraid to try. I don't like breaking things even if they're only small things.

But the really old ones are the ones who give trolls a dreadful name. It's not just occasional mischief, it's downright violent destruction that they love, and they slip out as often as they can to do damage. The ones between wild youth and rampaging old age—the middle-aged ones—try to keep some kind of control. It takes Mother and Father, Grandmother and Grandfather, and Great-g. and -g. to keep Great-great-g. and -g. from causing hysterical riots among you people. They are a total handful, because we trolls don't want you humans (Homo sapiens—we are Trollus superius) to know about us. Jorpaditch knows what you'd do to us if you found us out. We are greatly outnumbered. We might even end up in a zoo! So you can understand Father's concern when not only Great-great-g. and -g. are a care, but Great-g. and -g. are beginning to show their age—seven thousand years! Noise, throwing and breaking things, causing trouble among you humans in any sneaky way possible, has started with them, too.

Such naughty pranks. Floods, mud slides, earthquakes!

Father didn't ask me to come and help. I think he just felt the need to write a

complaining letter, to blow off smoke. But I
shall write at once and give what comfort and
advice I can. Though I can see down the
avenue that one day he, Mother, and G. and
G. won't be able to cope. Nor will they feel
free to ask my four brothers or five sisters to
come because they are at their raging youthful
best, all having a hilarious time under railroad
bridges. I'll have to go. I am the different one.
I am the one who worries himself into finding
quieter ways to do things. Well, it'll be a while
yet, so I'll not worry about it. As I always say
to myself, why worry about a thing today
when you have ten thousand years ahead of
you for it?

Oh, why did this come when the Gornuck
raised his slimy head?

Yesterday I called a meeting of rabbits and
frogs. (I didn't dare include foxes, ferrets,
and weasels at a rabbit meeting—I'll meet
with the others later.) I hoped we might be
able to join forces and devise some kind of
plan to chase away the Gornuck. I even
prepared carrots, parsley, and flies for them to
snack on. But can you believe it? The minute
I mentioned the Gornuck, they hopscotched
out through my doors and windows so fast, the
whole warren had vanished within two
minutes, frogs along with them! The flies I let
go. All these carrots to eat!

Well, for the moment I am quite safe from that monster. My house has a long, long hallway from the mailbox hole to my living room. Way back when, the Gornuck managed to squeeze through for that one dinner, but now that he is as big as he is, he could never make his way in. He is really no more than a nervous nuisance to me, as long as I'm careful, though I do think he's looking for me. I believe he's trying to remember which of the holes in the bank is my mailhole. I only have to remember to look through the mailhole before I venture out.

I want you to know too that there is no danger to you, either, because he only comes out at night to slodge around under the bridge. If Ritchie has another note from you, he should leave it under the rock in the *morning* before school, or *right* after school. I can see from my window if there's an edge of paper showing. Ritchie mustn't mess around in the dark.

> As always, your affectionate and
> ever honest troll, pod

p.s. It will probably take me a long time to answer Father's letter, so I may be a bit late in writing to you. Do forgive me.
p.p.s. I'd love to have another letter from you.

This was a *long* letter—almost like reading a book—and it took me a long time to read it to Rosie. I had to stop to explain a lot of things to her. There were words I wasn't sure of either, so after I read the letter through two more times, I wrote them down and told Rosie I'd look them up in the dictionary. Like "obstreperous" and "nuisances" and "hysterical" and "hilarious." I wrote down "prodigiously," too, from his other letter.

"I'm glad pod is safe from the Gornuck," Rosie said.

"So am I."

"I'm glad he won't go to the Pevurian Ands right away," she said.

"Peruvian," I said. "So am I."

"I'm glad he came to live with us," she said.

"Hey, he lives under Thad Grailowsky's bridge!" I said. But I knew what she meant. Somehow, with his letters in the drawer, the house didn't seem quite so empty.

Then I had to look up "Peruvian Andes," though I was pretty sure "Peruvian" came from "Peru," and I knew that was in South America. First I found it in the atlas, and I'd just found it on the globe when my father came home.

"Don't play with the globe," he said.

I used to like to spin it really fast when I was little.

"I'm not playing with it," I said. "I'm looking for something."

"Um," he said. "Well, don't play with it."

"I won't," I said, and went out to the kitchen to warm up supper on the stove. I'd already found where Peru was and that the Andes were mountains.

74

My father was reading the paper while we were eating leftover stew. I asked, "Are the Peruvian Ands really high?"

"The what?" my father asked.

"The Peruvian Ands."

"What are they?" my father asked.

"Mountains," I said.

"You mean the An*dees*," he said.

"Oh," I said, and felt stupid. Nobody had ever told me you said An*dees*, but I thought I should have known even if it didn't say in the atlas how to pronounce them. I didn't ask again how high they were and my father didn't tell me. I could find that out by myself.

But there were some other things I had to know, and I wanted to know now.

"Do they have mud slides and earthquakes in Peru?"

My father almost looked at me. "What?"

"Do they have mud slides and earthquakes in Peru?" I asked again.

"Look in the geology book," he said. He didn't say any more. He went back to reading the paper. My father knew a lot of things. He just never wanted to tell me. He always said, "Go look it up yourself," even when he knew.

All at once I was mad again. Thad Grailowsky would have looked at me. He would have said, "Yes. Bad ones." He would have asked, "Why?" And we would have talked.

I did the dishes and got the geology book out. It was a fat brown book with my grandfather's name in it. It had long words like "Mesozoic" and "Triassic" and "pyroxenites." But that wasn't what I was looking for. I looked up "earthquakes" and found some maps of where they were in the world. On page 345 it showed them across the whole middle of the other half of the world. When I turned the page, there was our side of the world. The whole side of South America was black with earthquakes! It was black where California was too.

Then I looked up volcanos. There was a double map of the whole world on page 375 with volcanos sprinkled all over. But there was a real mess of them from the bottom all the way up the west side of South America where Peru was, and then up the west side of North America and around Alaska and down through Japan and on down south of that.

If I had asked Thad Grailowsky, he would have told me all this. He would have said, "They have earthquakes in South America and California and Japan and New Guinea and Turkey. I don't know about mud slides."

"How about volcanos?" I would have asked. He would have told me.

Now I said, "Wow!" really loud. "Those trolls have moved all the way around the Pacific Ocean!"

My father was reading a book now. He looked up the way he does when he doesn't want to be bothered. "What did you say?"

"I said the . . ." I swallowed and thought fast. ". . . volcanos go all the way around the Pacific Ocean. Why do they do that?"

"Read the book."

I read for a while—what I could. The earthquakes went around too, just like the volcanos, only the two

76

earthquake maps weren't together, so I hadn't noticed that. After a while I said, "It doesn't say."

He said, "It's too complicated for you to understand. Go to bed."

I looked at him. Did that mean he didn't know either? Because I *did* understand. The book said they didn't know why.

But *I* knew why, and I went up to tell Rosie.

Trolls!

Eleven

I took Rosie to the bathroom first. I piggybacked her, because she could get there faster that way. I took her back to bed. *Then* I said, "Hey, Rosie, guess what?" And I told her.

Oh, her eyes were big and she was excited and she was smiling.

"They really are? Just like pod said?"

"Just like pod said."

"They make earthquakes and mud slides and volcanos and pod's our friend?"

"Yup!" I liked the way she said *our* friend, even if pod was really writing to her.

"I want to write him another letter!"

So I helped her do "DEAR pod." It was sort of crooked, but she made the letters herself even if the *E* was backward.

"What should I say?" she wanted to know.

"Whatever you want to."

She thought a long time and then her eyes got tears in them. "I don't know what!"

"Anything," I said.

At last she said, "Help me with 'I love you.' "

"Okay." I helped her with that. Then she did "rose-nander," copying it off his letter. We folded it in half and I put it with my arithmetic. "I'll put it under the rock before school," I told her.

My father called up the stairs. "Why are you keeping Rosie awake?"

Rosie smiled a secret smile at me and I went to my room.

I could hardly wait until morning to put that letter out for pod. I woke up once and wondered if it was almost morning. I got up and went to the bathroom and opened the bathroom window and looked out to see where a little piece of the moon was shining on the field. It was dark and quiet and mysterious. The trees growing in a row along the creek were black and fingery without their leaves. There were stars in the sky bigger than I'd ever seen them. An owl glided across the field without even flapping its wings. It didn't make a sound. It was all so different from the day that it made me hold my breath until I finally had to breathe just a little so I wouldn't die. I couldn't help but think about pod. It seemed like the world was full of . . . well, magic! I listened hard to hear if the Gornuck was slodging around in the creek under the bridge.

I wasn't sure. Maybe . . . just maybe, I heard something.

Then in the morning it was raining again. It wasn't coming down fat and hard the way it does with a thunderstorm so that you know in half an hour it'll be finished. No, it was coming down straight and thin, steady, clammy, and cold, solid gray and socked in and settled down to at least three days of it. As gloomy as any almost-November day could ever be. If I went through the field, I'd be wet up to my middle from the dead grass because the path wasn't mashed down to dirt the way it should be. If I went all the way around the block and in through Thad Grailowsky's place, I'd be late for school. Besides, the rocks would be all wet and the letter would get wet and pod wouldn't be able to read it.

I went in to see Rosie and tell her. She was sitting up looking out the window. Her underlip came out. She'd worked hard on that letter.

"I'll keep it in my jacket pocket until the rain stops," I told her, and folded it up small.

It was one of those soggy days when everything in school smells like wet wool and rubber and banana peels and feet and the red stuff the janitor shoves around on the floor with the big wide push broom. We had to stay in at noon and both recesses. Everybody kept getting noisier and noisier. When Miss Goodlatty went out of the room for a minute, we were all out of our seats and yelling and throwing spitballs and paper wads. When we heard her heels clacking in the hallway, we were all back in our seats in half a second.

The only other good part of the day was when Miss Goodlatty passed out extra manila paper after second recess and told us to take out our crayons. The kids who didn't have their own crayons got to take broken ones out of the shoe box full of them that Miss Goodlatty kept in the closet.

"We've already done Halloween decorations. Now I want you to draw something different. A picture out of your own head," Miss Goodlatty said while Sue Kolinsky took the box up and down the aisles so people could choose the colors they wanted. "It can be a scene from a book you've read, or something you've seen or heard about, or just something you imagine."

Most of the kids liked art. Even Melvin Collins liked to draw things. He couldn't draw very well, but you could always tell what it was. He always did a dog biting a mailman's arm off, really gory with a pail of red-crayon blood spilling all over the page. The kids sitting around him snickered when he took three red crayons out of the box.

Eddy Yordy always drew airplanes. I did too, some-times. Tony Cenuzzi drew the best in the class. One time when we had to draw each other, he drew Phyllis Kreuger. He had a crush on her. It was a really good picture. He'll probably be an artist when he grows up.

Today I didn't want to draw airplanes. It took me awhile to decide what to do. Then I drew the creek and the bridge and Thad Grailowsky's house. I put in trees and bushes. It was hard. I kept trying to think just how it looked, but I couldn't really remember all of it. What I didn't know, I sort of filled in. All the time I was thinking about pod and Rosie and all the things pod had told her in his letters.

Miss Goodlatty walked up and down the aisles looking over our shoulders. After a while she said it was time to stop.

"We'll talk about our pictures now," she said. "You'll each come up to the front of the room and tell the others what you drew and why you drew it."

Everybody groaned, but that didn't make Miss Goodlatty change her mind. She started with Patsy Gruen, who sat in the first seat in the first row. She'd drawn a girl pushing a doll buggy. She said it was her little sister, only she didn't have a doll buggy. She just wanted one. Everybody told something. It was somebody from their favorite book, or a horse, or their house, or a jar of flowers. Eddy Yordy drew an airplane dropping bombs. Melvin Collins told us his was a bull trampling on a matador. We'd talked about Spain and bullfights yesterday. There was red blood all over, but it wasn't the mailman, anyway.

When it came to my turn, I said it was the field and trees back of our house. Then I had to say why, so I said, "It's for Rosie because she's a little better, but she can't go out there yet."

Then Sue Kolinsky said, "It's got the bridge where she pretends the troll lives. Does she still pretend that?"

I swallowed. "Yeah," I said. "She can't really see the bridge, so she can look at the picture."

"Geez! Dumb!" Melvin Collins said. "Whyn'cha put the troll in eatin' her?"

"It's a nice picture, Ritchie, but I don't know if it's a good idea for a little girl to think about a troll," Miss Goodlatty said. "I should think she would be very frightened by it. She should think about happy things when she's sick this way."

I went to my seat. I looked at Miss Goodlatty, but I didn't say anything. Miss Goodlatty didn't know anything about my sister. But I knew something about my teacher right away. Miss Goodlatty wasn't writing those letters!

It rained really hard all day Wednesday and all day Thursday, too. When I took the milk bottle to set out on the porch after supper Thursday night, snow was coming down. Wet, soggy snow that melted on the driveway. I held out my hand to catch some big flakes and watch them melt. When I looked out my bedroom window, the snow looked black around the streetlight at the corner.

I hoped there'd be lots of snow in the morning, but it had mostly melted. Only little clumps of it showed where it was caught in the long brown grass in the field. Dark clouds with lumpy gray in them ran low across the sky, and it was freezing cold. If it didn't snow again, I hoped by the time school was out it might be dry enough to put Rosie's letter under the stone by the bridge.

Being Friday, it was Melvin Collins's turn to write Rosie a letter. He gave me an awful look, and all at once I remembered I'd forgotten to put my glasses in the case after school for three days. I'd better do it today.

Melvin Collins worked on something for a while and then stamped up the aisle to show it to Miss Goodlatty.

"That's fine, Melvin," she said, and handed it back to him.

I put my glasses away after school. I ran the first block and a half toward home. Then I stopped to put my glasses on because Melvin Collins always caught me at the first corner and he hadn't caught me today. I looked at his letter. Right away I knew it wasn't the one he'd showed to Miss Goodlatty. This one said:

Dear dum Rosie
   Yor as crazy as yor mother. Thers no trol
under the brij.

I started to tear it up and then I wondered if I should. Rosie would be expecting her Friday letter. I couldn't read her this one, but neither could she. Maybe I could make up something and pretend to read it off the paper. I stuffed the letter in my pocket and walked on ice-skin puddles on the sidewalk. If the puddle was deep, the ice would break. If there was just a little water under it, it would sort of bend and squeak. I always liked that. I didn't find many puddles. The sidewalk was mostly dry.

I wondered if the rock under the bridge was dry. I'd go around the long way to find out. If it was, I'd leave Rosie's letter. That gave me a chance to find more ice-skin puddles.

I never looked behind me once.

Twelve

I turned off the sidewalk onto the path that ran along the creek beside Thad Grailowsky's house. I'd stop and say hello to Thad Grailowsky after I left the letter.

It still looked wet in the dead grass under the bridge where the big rock was. I went down the bank a little way to make sure. The creek was running high and fast from all the rain, but it was an easy slope on this side and I could get down right to the edge of the water.

No, it was too wet to leave Rosie's letter.

I climbed back up and then I thought of something. I mean I really wondered. I *had* to try to see, so I went up on the bridge to look. I couldn't see anything from there because the hole had to be *under* the bridge. Maybe I could see from the bank on the other side. That bank was high and steep because of the way the creek curved and washed it out underneath, but I was careful. I went through the grass along the edge to where I thought I could see, and stooped down.

That was a mistake.

Because Melvin Collins had followed me.

I didn't know until right then when I heard him running across the bridge. I stood up fast with the most awful feeling of being afraid that I'd ever had in my life.

I don't know exactly how it happened. I remember pushing and shoving and kicking and hanging on to him—the feeling of his jacket in my hands. And then the feeling of sliding on my back, my jacket curling up so my shirt was in the mud, down the bank into the creek. The cold water filled up my boots and came up above the top of my legs.

I turned around quick to grab at something on the bank to hold on to. There was nothing but one slimy root. The rest was mud. I grabbed the root with one hand and I dug my fingers of my other hand into the mud.

Then I heard Melvin Collins yell, "Hey, four-eyes. How's that for a big one? If you don't think it's enough, I've got more!"

I looked up. There were two other kids with Melvin. They were all looking down at me, but I was too scared to say anything. Then they all turned around and ran.

All I could think was that I had to get out. It was so cold. I tried to climb but it was slick mud and the few handholds of grass I grabbed just pulled out. It seemed to get more and more slippery. There was a tree branch hanging down not far from me and I stepped a little sideways. But the creek was deeper there and I went into a hole right up to my middle. It was lucky I was still holding on to the root. My legs were slow and the water pulled at me so, it took forever to get back just two steps.

Then I stood there with the water pulling at me, and looked up and down the creek. Both ways the bank on this side got higher. I could have gotten out on the other side of the creek where the bank was low, where the rock was for the letter, but with all the rain, the middle of the creek was deep and running fast. It would be over my head. If it had been summer—but it wasn't summer. I had all my clothes on and the water was cold. I didn't dare try to cross. I didn't know where I could get out. Oh, it was cold. My fingers were already stiff.

There must have been a little break in the clouds just then, because a spot of pale yellow sun showed through the bare trees. In a minute it was gone again. That sun was low and would be down in no time. It would be dark and I was getting colder and colder. What if . . . what if the Gornuck came?

Why didn't pod come and pull me out?

I thought of the culvert and the way the creek was roaring through it and foaming against the top of it.

Didn't I know? Didn't I really know about pod?

Darned old pretend troll!

Help! I wanted to yell. *Help!* And I opened my mouth. But it was just a little noise: "Help." I almost thought I heard a kitten meowing. Nobody could ever hear that!

"Help." I tried again, all of the sound of it staying high inside my throat. It doesn't matter, I thought, because there was nobody around to hear me anyway.

Then I heard Thad Grailowsky's little white dog barking. I could see her face on the bridge just above me. *Yap yap yap! Yap yap yap! Yap yap yap!* Her ears pointed forward.

I dug my fingers deeper into the mud of the bank, hung on to the one slippery root, and looked up at her, wishing she could get me out.

Yap yap yap! Yap yap yap! Yap yap yap! Looking down at me. Yapping forever!

Just when I thought "forever," she looked aside and ran away. I started to cry.

Then Thad Grailowsky was looking over the side of the bridge.

"Ritchie!"

He was around the end of the bridge and on the bank. He didn't bother that my hands were all cold and wet and muddy. He just got a good foothold, grabbed my wrists, and pulled me out.

He ran me to his shack. I mean my legs were moving but it seemed like my feet weren't always on the ground.

He pushed me into the house and pulled off my jacket and boots. My shoes came off inside my boots, full of water and mud. He dropped them on the floor. There was a fire in the barrel stove, but I thought if I walked over close to it, I'd get the floor all wet. I stood and shivered.

"Take off your wet stuff," he said, and started the water running in the sink.

I was so cold, I could hardly move. I pushed my trousers off, but my fingers were too cold to unbutton my shirt buttons. He had to help. He set a stool in front of the sink for me to stand on and made me put my hands and arms in the hot water. He filled a basin with hot water too and picked up my feet while I leaned against the sink and shoved it under them on the stool and put them down in it. Then he got the biggest towel I'd ever seen and warmed it for a few seconds right on the barrel stove. When he wrapped it around me, I thought I'd never felt anything so good.

"Now rub yourself dry," he told me, and went and got a blanket. He warmed that, too, and when I said I was dry, he wrapped me up in the blanket, like putting me in a sack, and sat me in a chair by the stove. Then he called Mrs. Cavanaugh on the telephone.

"This is Thad Grailowsky. Ritchie fell in the creek. You'd better bring over some dry clothes right away."

He held the receiver away from his ear, and I could hear the squawking all the way across the room.

"Okay," he said after a minute, and hung up.

He brought a hot-water bottle and a pair of his socks because my bare feet were sticking out the end of the blanket. "Kind of late in the year for swimming," he said while he filled the bottle.

"Ye-eah," I said. The socks were way too big. I pulled the heel parts up the back of my legs. He gave me the hot-water bottle and I took it inside the blanket and put it on my lap and rested my arms on top of it.

He poured some milk into a pan and set it on the stove. "I heard Pooch barking," he said. "She does that a lot. She goes on the bridge and barks. Sometimes it's a cat or maybe a water rat. But when she kept on that long I wondered if there was something there I ought to see about."

"I'm glad she kept barking," I said.

"I was wondering about keeping Pooch," he went on. "I'd rather have a big dog." He leaned down and patted her head and said, "Good Pooch." The dog rolled over on her back, her skinny tail wagging at the tip. You knew she was still afraid to wag it all the way up. Thad Grailowsky rubbed her stomach with his foot while he poured the milk into a cup. Her ribs didn't show the way they had at first.

"I saw some kids on the road," he said, and stirred chocolate syrup into the milk and handed me the cup.

"Ye-eah?" I said, and wrapped both my hands around the hot cup.

When I didn't say any more, he asked, "How's Rosie?"

"Better," I said, and tasted the hot chocolate. It was warm and sweet and thick and spread downward and sideways inside me. Then Mrs. Cavanaugh was at the door. She'd come through the field.

I don't know what all she said.

When we got home, she told me she couldn't stay, but I should soak in hot water. So after I said hi to Rosie, I soaked. I kept running more hot water into the tub until the hot got right through inside my bones. I was still soaking when my father got home.

He had to warm up the supper himself.

Thirteen

Saturday morning I stayed in bed. I wasn't sick. I just didn't want to get up. I didn't even want to read—not even *The Count of Monte Cristo*. Suddenly I remembered my glasses. What if they had fallen out of my jacket pocket into the creek?

"Why aren't you up?" My father's voice made me almost jump out of bed. Mrs. Cavanaugh told me I'd have to tell him what happened. I hadn't. Why should I? I hadn't drowned. But if I'd lost my glasses . . .

Now I told a lie. "I think I've got a cold."

"Um," he said. "Keep an eye on Rosie when I go shopping." He went back downstairs.

But before he went shopping, I heard the doorbell ring. It couldn't be Aunt Vickie. She didn't ring the bell. She always opened the door and said, "Hallo!" really loud, and started talking. I had to go to the bathroom just then, so I was near the top of the stairs when my father opened the door.

It was Thad Grailowsky's voice. I noticed how it sounded kind of like his cello. He'd brought my clothes over. My father didn't ask him to come in. They stood in the doorway and talked. I couldn't tell what they were saying, except once when Thad Grailowsky's voice got loud. "You ought to ask him," he said. Then he went away and my father closed the door.

I ran back down the hall on my tiptoes and jumped into my bed and pulled the blanket over my head. I didn't want him to ask me. I kept waiting for him to come and ask. Then I heard the car go out the driveway, so I knew he'd gone shopping. I kicked the blanket off.

"I didn't *want* him to ask me," I said out loud. I stayed there for a while, listening to nothing. Everything seemed sad all over again. Even with pod's letters in the house it was sad, because pod wasn't . . .

"So he isn't," I said.

Then I decided I wouldn't talk to my father anymore. I'd never bother him again. I'd say "Um" if he ever said anything to me.

Then I said—I don't know why, because I wasn't thinking about that now—I whispered, "There's no more magic."

After that I got up and got dressed and went to see how Rosie was.

Last night I hadn't told her what happened. Now I did.

"I wonder if pod saw you get pushed?" she asked.

"Maybe."

"Maybe if Thad Grailowsky hadn't pulled you out, pod would have."

"Maybe," I said. I couldn't tell her pod wasn't real anymore.

"You could have been there all night. What if the Gornuck came?"

"I thought about that," I said.

"I'd have been scared." Rosie looked at me as if she thought I was brave. Then her under lip came out. "You didn't give pod his letter. Poor pod. He's been waiting and waiting for a letter."

"He knows it's been raining. Thad Grailowsky brought my jacket back. Maybe it's still in the pocket. If it's not all wet, I'll take it to the rock today," I said. I felt silly about leaving it for a pretend troll, but why should I spoil it for Rosie?

I went downstairs. Thad Grailowsky had cleaned the mud off my jacket. It was a leather jacket with pockets high up on the chest part. I was afraid to feel inside them, but I had to. My glasses were there.

I found Melvin Collins's letter too and squeezed it into a little damp wad and threw it into the wastebasket. Rosie's letter was damp. I took it upstairs and we unfolded it. We could still read it. I spread it out in front of the register to dry while we talked some more. When the paper was dry, she folded it up again, and I took it across the field and left it under the rock on this side of the bridge. I hoped Thad Grailowsky didn't see me. I got back before my father came home.

When he did, he didn't ask if my cold was better, so I couldn't say "Um."

On Sunday afternoon my father went to see Aunt

Vickie about something, so I had to stay with Rosie. I was reading her the funnies when she fell asleep, so I went downstairs and turned the radio on. The New York Philharmonic was playing. I finished the funnies on the living-room floor the way I used to. All at once I thought our mother was there. I looked at her chair, but she wasn't sitting in it. Maybe if I wished really hard, she would be there. I closed my eyes and wished. But she still wasn't there.

"Because there's no more magic," I whispered again, and felt sad all over again.

I wondered if she could listen to the radio in the hospital. She would like that. She wouldn't feel bad about the world and shake from a nervous breakdown if she could listen to the music.

Then it was the end of the program. I went upstairs. Rosie was awake and had gone to the bathroom by herself. After that I finished reading her the funnies.

At supper I was careful not to say anything to my father. I didn't have to tell him, because I'd found my glasses. Why should I bother him? When I went to bed, I still felt sad. It made my stomach hurt.

Monday at school Melvin Collins looked at me in a funny way. Was he surprised I wasn't drowned? Was he thinking about another big one? Did he want to kill me? So what? If I didn't care, it didn't matter. He could do whatever he wanted, but none of it would matter. I only looked at him once, and then I didn't look at him anymore all day. I just felt sad. When I wondered if Rosie would get a letter that afternoon, I didn't get excited. I thought, who cares? And felt even worse.

But there was one in the mailbox.

Who was writing them? Aunt Vickie? I didn't think so. Uncle Len? No. He was a man too. Some lady? Miss Minns, the second-grade teacher? Maybe, if Miss Good-latty had told her about Rosie. Miss Minns always thought of nice things to do for kids. Yeah, probably it was her.

I took the letter up to Rosie and started to read it:

> *Dear rosenander,*
>
> *And you too, Ritchie. I'm going to scold you. You must NEVER go down on that side of the creek. You don't know how it frightened me to see you alone in the water with evening coming on. The Gornuck could have been there any minute and swallowed you whole. No one would ever have found hide nor hair of you. If that wretched little dog hadn't kept up its incessant yapping, that's just what would have happened, because even if you're not very big, I'm not big enough to pull you out.*
>
> *Small creatures have so much trouble! If only big ones understood!*

I stopped and read that over again to myself. What was Miss Minns trying to do? Make excuses for pod not being real?

"Don't stop! Go on!" Rosie said.

I took a deep breath and went on:

> *And that little dog! I haven't liked it very much. It comes out and barks at me every time I go out for a day-stroll. You don't catch it*

coming out in the evening and barking at the
Gornuck, though. If it did, I'd be warned. No,
all day long it barks at everything else, even
sticks floating down the creek.

You should have heard it when I had a
meeting of weasels and ferrets and foxes day
before yesterday! A real annoyance. At least
the dog did help you by bringing the Man, so
it had some use and I suppose I will have to
learn to tolerate it.

As for the meeting, it was as unsuccessful as
the one with the rabbits and frogs. The
weasels—nine of them—snarled and hissed at
the foxes—seven of them—and ate everything
in sight, while the ferrets got into my
cupboards and ice box. Then they had the
nerve to tell me the Gornuck was my problem.
They could look after themselves, thank you.
Was there anything more to eat? No. Good-
bye! And they were gone.

The foxes shrugged and nibbled, and used
their napkins very neatly, looking superior as
usual. Only the oldest—Grandpère Renard—
had advice.

"Of course you built too close to zee
rivaire," he said, and smoothed his whiskers
back with his paw. "I always thought so. Now
you mus' leave."

"But I don't want to run away!" I said.

He shrugged. "Zen you weel be eaten."

They all shrugged, washed their paws, and left. No help at all!

Now, to other things.

Did you read about the earthquake in Chile earlier this year? A huge one. Not my g. and g.'s, though. Another branch of the family there.

You notice they don't get earthquakes and volcanos in western Europe. There are lots of railroads, and trolls do live there, but there are so many people around that except for an occasional flood, fire, or ice storm we trolls stay under the bridges. But, there is a branch of the family that likes getting involved in their wars.

It is a dreadful branch of the family—the Bratch Bunch Branch. (When I say that too fast, sometimes it comes out the Bratch Bench Brunch!) They used to push me around when I was wangietroll (a very young troll). They'd throw me off bridges, lock me in dark caves. How I feared and hated them!

Now they live where the Orient Express crosses the Danube. By the news from there, I'm afraid they're in it again. Up to no good. They'll cause real troll trouble. I'm so worried! Somehow I must do something about them, but what? Oh dear, there are so many things to cope with, I'm not sure I can! The Gornuck, the wild g. and g.'s, the Bratch Bunch Branch . . . Then I remember Mother's words. She was full of wisdom.

"Don't take them all on at once. Smack one of them down, and you'll feel good about taking a fire hose to a fire." She loved going to fires, and fell in love with fire hoses a few hundred years ago. They make such wonderful steam and sizzlings when they put out fires! Of course they can't put them out if one of the Bratch Bunch Branch is there feeding drums of oil and old logs to an impossible conflagration.

Mother also found that a good stiff stream from a fire hose gave the great-great-g. and -g's. such a back scratching, they'd stay out of mischief for months. Old trolls have very itchy backs. Maybe that's what drives them to causing trouble.

Oh dear, fire hoses are not the point here. Troubles are. Meeting them one at a time. It's the best way to cope. But now and then you get one you can't cope with. It's too big. Like the Gornuck.

Mother had something for that, too. "Sometimes you have to take care of things by yourself. Krinkaws, goolibits, driddlepads— what have you. You have to find out how to do it and then go about doing it. But if they are too big and pile up so deep that however much you try to cope, you can't, *that's* when you need a big troll hand. There's nothing shameful about asking for one."

Of course I'm small, and she was trying to comfort me when everyone picked on me. But Mother isn't here now, and I am learning something else. Sometimes nobody can do anything about it!

I wonder. Is doing the best I can to look after myself the only way of coping? Maybe. Yet I keep asking, Why? why? why?

Why does he plague such a small one as me?

Why won't he talk to me, so I know what he wants?

Does he really not like me?

Suddenly I have a thought. Maybe he is jealous because he never learned to have fun! He never laughs (I don't think he cries, either) and doesn't want anyone else to do it! Maybe, just maybe, there was something during that dinner he had here that he enjoyed. Maybe he thinks if he has the place and me to work for him he will have that nice feeling—as if someone cared about him. Of course he won't have it because he doesn't care about me or anyone else. Poor thing—but still a monster! I will not be a slave to such a one!

Well, I wrote to you in the first place because I needed someone I knew cared. Now I have someone. And I want you both to know that I care about you.

Ritchie, you must promise me that you won't go down that bank trying to see my

mailbox hole, because I'm sure that's what you
were up to. And rosenander, do let me know
that he promises, and you must promise to get
better.

Your ever faithful and honest troll, pod

p.s. Thank you, thank you, thank you,
rosenander, for the beautiful letter. It has
made my whole life worthwhile.
p.p.s. I think your mother would like to have a
letter from you. Why don't you write a letter
to her just like the one you wrote to me?

I read the letter to Rosie three times over. The first time I just read it. The second time I started feeling strange about it. The third time two things really made me feel funny. How could Miss Minns know about Melvin Collins pushing me into the creek and about Thad Grailowsky's dog barking? She couldn't have seen us. She didn't live around here. I hadn't told anybody, and I was sure Melvin Collins hadn't either.

There were those two other boys—sixth graders. But why should they tell the second-grade teacher? How could anybody know?

Thad Grailowsky—*might* he be the one? But he was a man! And he *couldn't* spell, I told myself again. He'd *said* so. Those letters were spelled right. And he hated to write letters. He'd *said* so.

Oh, gosh! Had pod really seen me? Was I wrong? Was he really there? It made me feel so funny, I didn't want to think about it.

The other thing that made me feel strange was the p.p.s. Write a letter to our mother? We'd never thought of that! Where would we send it?

I'd have to do what I said I wouldn't do. I'd have to ask my father.

Fourteen

I decided I'd ask him at breakfast time. It shouldn't bother him while he was frying eggs. I thought and thought about what I would say so I wouldn't use too many words.

"Rosie and I want to write a letter to our mother. I need her address, please." I felt strange saying it. As if I was standing in the gymnasium, giving a speech to the whole school.

"Um. Why?" he asked. "Rosie can't write."

I'd thought he might say no and I'd ask why not. Instead, *he* was asking why, and I didn't know what to say. I couldn't tell him a troll told us to!

I said, "Because we want to. I'll show Rosie how."

He put the eggs on the plates. Mine could have bounced, and it was brown and hard around the edges. I don't like an egg that way.

When he didn't say anything, I said, "Because maybe our mother would like it."

He ate some egg and toast and drank some coffee. Then he said, "Write the letter. I'll mail it."

"I know how to write an envelope," I said.

"I'll do it," he said.

"Um," I said, without opening my mouth.

Before I went to school, I went upstairs and told Rosie we'd write a letter to our mother after I got home. Rosie got all excited and happy about it.

But I didn't feel good about it. If my father mailed the letter, I still wouldn't know which hospital our mother was in. If he wanted to, he could read what we'd written, and I didn't want him to know. I couldn't write her a letter all by myself and mail it without telling him about it.

What was the matter that he couldn't tell me her address? Then I thought, How can I be so dumb? Aunt Vickie was in the hospital once and our mother had called up on the telephone to ask how she was. *I* could call up the hospital and ask how our mother was! Like pod said in his letter. Sometimes you have to do things yourself. You have to find out how to do it and then go ahead and do it.

I hated calling grown-up people on the telephone, but I *had* to do this.

Which hospital? What if I called the wrong one? I hated to be wrong, too. But I *had* to try. If she wasn't in the first one, I'd say, "I'm sorry, I must have the wrong hospital." I wouldn't tell them who it was. Then I'd call the other one. I'd do it as soon as I got home.

Now *I* was excited. We could write to our mother because we'd know where she was!

That was the longest day I'd ever had in school. When I

got home, as soon as Mrs. Cavanaugh was gone I looked up the telephone number for St. Mary's hospital. I took a deep breath. My heart was beating really hard when I said I wanted to know how Mrs. Myra Willis was. The lady said, "One moment, please." Then after a few minutes, she said, "We don't have a patient by that name." I said thank you and I was sorry. Then I called the other hospital. I was so excited I could hardly talk.

But when the lady said she wasn't there, my hand was so heavy all of a sudden it couldn't hold up the receiver. I hung up. I don't know if I said thank you or I was sorry or what. All my insides were gone. Where was our mother? Was she really in the hospital? Maybe when you had a nervous breakdown they put you in jail. How did I know?

I could hear Rosie calling me. What would I tell her? Had pod said anything else to help me? He said you have to cope. You have to face the Gornuck. You have to take care of the g. and g.'s. You have to go and fight the Bratch Bunch Branch. Start with one brave thing and go on to the next. Well, I'd started by trying to find out where our mother was, and it only made things worse.

Then I thought, pod's problems are sort of like mine, except he knows where his mother is. The rest of it—the Gornuck, the g. and g.'s, the Bratch Bunch Branch . . .

I have to talk to my father.

I have to take care of Rosie.

I have to tell Melvin Collins he can't have another big one—or else I have to fight him. There's no way I can run away from him.

How could I ever fight Melvin Collins? What would ever make me brave enough to do that?

Pod said knowing Rosie was his friend made him brave. I didn't have a friend to make me feel brave. I had Rosie, but she was my sister. That's different. I had Len Junior and Gordy, and I liked them, but they were my cousins and called me twerp. My best friend at school, Don Bowes, was in the fourth grade. Now I didn't see him much at all because I always had to come home. I didn't have any friends in the fifth grade. Oh, Sue Kolinsky was a little bit friendly, but she wasn't really a *friend* friend. I didn't know her outside of school. All I really had in the fifth grade was my worst enemy, and he should be in the sixth grade!

I thought a long time about that. Then I thought. Thad Grailowsky is my friend. I'm going to talk to him. I'll tell him our mother *isn't* in the hospital.

Then I had a terrible thought, and I started getting scared. Where *was* our mother? What if . . . ? It was the most awful feeling I'd ever had. I couldn't even think about it.

My hands and feet felt all heavy. I went upstairs to help Rosie write the letter. Rosie said, "Dear Mama, I love you. Rosie." She wanted to say "rosenander," but I told her our mother wasn't a troll. I wrote on the same paper and told our mother that school was okay now and we wished she was home. I couldn't think of anything else. I was so empty. Then I read to Rosie.

When my father came home, I gave him the letter and he said he'd mail it. Where would he send it?

I had to ask. "Will she get it? Is she alive?"

"Of course she is!"

I could tell he was really angry with me. But that wasn't

why I ran upstairs to my bedroom. That wasn't why I cried and hit my pillow and hit it and hit it and hit it. I don't know why I did that, but after a while I felt better.

After school on Wednesday I went to talk to Thad Grailowsky, but he wasn't home. Mrs. Cavanaugh wanted me home right after school on Thursday and Friday, so I couldn't see him. On Saturday, I had to stay with Rosie most of the day. Then it was Sunday.

Aunt Vickie came over with Uncle Len and all five cousins. Mary Alice and Patsy and Margaret went up to see Rosie. Len Junior and Gordy and I went out to look for something to do. We were dropping sticks into the creek on one side of the culvert and running across the street to see if they'd come out on the other side when a car with Illinois license plates drove up and parked in front of Thad Grailowsky's shack. Three men got out. They had dark overcoats and hats on. They carried violin cases. One of the cases was bigger than the other two. One of the men had a briefcase, too. They went into the house without even knocking. Just pushed open the door and went in.

Cousin Len sucked in loud. Then he whispered, "Gangsters! They got tommy guns!"

"Nah!" I said. "They got violins."

"Yeah, yeah, twerp! Violins!" Gordy nodded his head like he knew everything.

"Yeah, violins!" I said.

"Tommy guns! They always carry them in violin cases. If you think you're so smart, whyn't you go and see?" Len Junior asked.

106

"Go ahead and look yourself," I said. "I don't look in people's windows."

"Nah, go knock on the door. You're not afraid of a few tommy guns are you, twerp? How much you wanna bet they got money from a bank robbery in that briefcase?"

All of a sudden I wasn't sure. How did I know they were violins, just because they were violin cases?

"G'wan! Show us how brave you are, twerp."

"All right!" I said. "Quit pushing me." I started walking toward his shack.

Wasn't Thad Grailowsky my friend? Didn't I help him bury Blackie?

Yes, but . . . And hadn't he pulled me out of the creek? Yes, but . . . One thing at a time, Ritchie, pod said. One brave thing . . .

If he was really my friend, Thad Grailowsky could always open the door just a little and tell me to scram and close the door quick so I couldn't see the tommy guns.

I swallowed hard. I was already there with my knuckles up in front of the door. What should I do? Then my hand started knocking on the door.

The door opened. It was Thad Grailowsky. I waited for him to tell me to scram, but he didn't.

"Hey, Ritchie!" he said. "What brings you here? Come on in!" He took my arm and pulled me into the house and closed the door behind me.

Those three men had taken off their coats and hats. They sure filled up the room. One of them looked a little bit like James Cagney out of the movies.

"This is Ritchie Willis. Myra Willis's kid. You remember the time we played the Trout Quintet with her?"

They all looked at me.

"Myra Willis! Sure. And we did the Brahms F minor, too! What a pianist! And what fun she was! Hey, when was that? A long time. Four—five years ago? We should do it again! Why don't you ask her?"

"She's been busy," Thad Grailowsky said.

I was glad he didn't tell them she had a nervous breakdown. By then of course I'd seen the violin case that was open and had a violin in it, just like I'd said it would. I took a deep breath and let it out.

"Do you play, Ritchie?" one of them asked.

"I started on the piano," I said.

"We're playing quartets this afternoon," Thad Grailowsky said. "Do you want to stay and listen?"

"Just a little while," I said. "My cousins are here today."

They were setting up music stands and taking out their instruments—the big one was a viola—and tightening their bows and tuning up. Thad Grailowsky set the end pin of his cello in a notch in the floor and played some notes. I sat on the couch. They had all the chairs.

One of them opened the briefcase. It had music in it. They decided on Beethoven.

I didn't mean to stay so long. It was just that once they started, it sounded like nothing else I'd ever heard, and I was right in the middle of it. It filled me up right to my chin.

Sometimes they'd stop and argue, or laugh about some-

108

thing, especially the viola that had a new C string on it that kept going flat. The violist would make a face and tune it. Then they'd start in again. I knew I should get up and say I had to leave, but I didn't want to. So I didn't.

They played a lot. They'd stopped to rest a few minutes when there was a knock at the door.

Thad Grailowsky went to answer it.

"I'm looking for Richard Willis!" Aunt Vickie's voice was louder than I'd ever heard it. She looked around the edge of Thad Grailowsky to see what was going on.

"Sure! He's here," said Thad Grailowsky, turning around. "You're wanted, Ritchie!"

But I was already on my feet.

"Nice to meet you, Ritchie," the second violin called after me.

I looked back. "Yeah," I said. "Yeah, sure. Thanks." I felt my mouth grinning so wide it pushed my ears back.

Fifteen

I was never so embarrassed in my life!" Aunt Vickie yelled and grabbed Len Junior by the ear.

"Gee whiz! Ouch! How did we know? We waited and waited and he never came out. We thought they'd kidnapped him!" Len Junior howled.

"We figured he was tied up to a chair or dead or something," Gordy said. "Gangsters with tommy guns! Boy, I wouldn't have gone into that house for a million dollars!"

"I don't know why you should be embarrassed, Aunt Vickie," I said. "You just asked for me to come home."

She let go of Len Junior's ear.

"Well!" She huffed and hunched her shoulders up and down as if to straighten out all her underwear. "How did I know but what there were a bunch of Chicago mobsters in there."

"They play in the Chicago Symphony Orchestra," I

said. "They're awful good. They know Thad Grailowsky from when he took cello lessons in Chicago."

Aunt Vickie huffed and hunched around a little more and then said they'd better be getting home.

While they were going out the door, I said, "It was awful brave of you to go in where you thought there were a bunch of Chicago mobsters, Aunt Vickie. If I'd needed help, you'd have been right there."

"Well!" she said again. Then she looked more cheerful. "You keep an eye on him, Edward," she said to my father. "Falling in the creek one day and going in where there might be mobsters the next! There's no telling what he'll do. All those brains and no sense at all!"

I didn't feel very good about what she said, but Len Junior and Gordy were looking at me differently. I didn't mind that, except inside I knew it wasn't that way at all. Sure I'd like everybody to think I was brave, but how did you go about *really* being brave? I mean, getting pushed into the creek and standing there meowing like a cat wasn't really brave!

Even so, I was feeling pretty good about myself for a change.

Then my father spoiled it.

After Aunt Vickie left, he said, "I want you to stay away from Thad Grailowsky."

I couldn't believe what he'd said. "Why?" I asked. "He only plays music."

"I know that," he said. "I don't want you to bother him."

"I don't bother him!"

"Just stay away."

I didn't say anything. I didn't even say "Um." I'd forgotten all about it. I went upstairs and sat on my bed. It seemed like the floor all around me had turned into a big black hole. Why wouldn't he let me have a friend? He wouldn't let me do anything! He wouldn't let anybody do anything! He didn't even want our mother to play the piano, and she was good enough for those people from the Chicago Symphony to want her to play with them! I bet he wouldn't *let* her do it! I'll bet he said, "I don't want you to bother them." Then I thought, our mother didn't have any friends either except Aunt Vickie, and Aunt Vickie just talked about where people bought their clothes and how much pork chops cost in the IGA store. She never said anything about music having a sound that shivered all the way through inside you!

I didn't say anything the next morning at breakfast. I set the salt and pepper where we could both reach it so I wouldn't have to ask for it. My father didn't notice. He took the salt, and after he'd sprinkled it on his eggs, he set it down beside his plate. I wouldn't ask for it. I ate mine without any salt. He didn't say anything the whole time, so I didn't have a chance to say "Um."

On the way to school I decided I'd run away. Where would I run to? Should I go down to the railroad tracks at the switchyard and hang around with some hobos?

I thought of the tramp who had come to our house a couple of years ago and asked for food. He was thin and old and had really blue eyes. Our mother let him eat in the kitchen. Then she gave him an old overcoat of my father's. I wondered if there was a mark on our house that let tramps know they could get something to eat here. I looked and looked for it, but I couldn't find anything. I wondered when I ran away, if I would get old and skinny and ragged—would I know where to look for a mark on a house? If I came to our house, would my father know who I was? Would he be sorry?

Then I remembered Rosie. I'd promised her I'd never go away. Who would read to her? Who would help her write a letter to pod?

Pod! Maybe there'd be a letter from him today! Maybe I should write to him and ask him what to do! Of course he had his own troubles. Besides, I'd decided there wasn't any ... But even so, maybe ... *Somebody* was writing those letters to Rosie! Why not pod?

All right! If I couldn't talk to Thad Grailowsky, I'd write to pod and ask him what I should do!

I thought about it off and on in school. Somehow knowing what I was going to do made me think better. I was in a hurry about everything. I finished the arithmetic problems on the board so fast I guess Miss Goodlatty thought I was cheating. But I couldn't be, because she'd made up the problems herself. I always remember everything I read, so when she asked me, I answered right away. I couldn't waste time pretending not to know the answers in school so Melvin Collins wouldn't call me Mr. Know-it-all.

I didn't know what was eating Melvin Collins, because

at afternoon recess, he pushed against me and said, "You creep!" But he didn't push me down, and he didn't say anything about another big one, so it didn't bother me.

I could hardly wait for school to be out. I was in a hurry to get home and see if there was a letter from pod. I almost ran down the steps, though we weren't supposed to run. I ran to the corner.

There was Melvin Collins with those two sixth graders, waiting for me.

"Little Ritchie! Teacher's pet!" he yelled, and before I could think anything, he grabbed me. But he didn't push me down. He pulled my glasses off and threw them down in front of me and stamped on them. I heard the awful crunch.

For a second, there was no sound in the whole world. It was all dark and still. Then it turned red. Then I think I yelled. I put my head down and yelled. I could see enough to see Melvin Collins standing in front of me. I put my head down and yelled and ran at him.

Thunk! It was hard and soft at the same time. There was a strange noise like steam out of train-engine pistons and there was Melvin Collins on his back on the sidewalk. I jumped on him and started to hit. I hit and I hit. Just like I did the pillow. There was a lot of noise then. Yelling and yelling and more yelling. And I just kept hitting. I didn't know where, but I knew how and I knew who. All the time there was yelling.

Then somebody was grabbing my arms and hauling me off. I thought it was the sixth graders, but it was Mr. Genovo, the gym teacher.

"Ritchie! Stop it! Stop it!" he kept saying. When I

knew it was him, I stopped. There were other teachers around and Miss Mieres, the principal. By then Melvin Collins was on his feet too. A teacher was holding his arm. He was making funny sucking blubbery sounds. I wondered what was the matter with him. I'd have hit him some more if Mr. Genovo had let me go. But he was hauling me somewhere.

We were in the office. Melvin Collins and the two sixth graders and Mr. Genovo and Miss Mieres and three other teachers and the school nurse, Miss Goldberg. She'd been to our school that afternoon and was still there—in her dark blue dress and blue stockings and with her dark blue hat on. She always took her hat off when she looked down our throats and at our arms. I always wondered what she looked for on our arms.

They sat us on chairs next to each other and the nurse started looking us over. Miss Mieres was saying, "I'll have to call your fathers. Both of them."

Then I couldn't believe it, because Melvin Collins and I both yelled at the same time. "No! No! Don't call my old man! Don't call my father!"

"I have to," Miss Mieres said.

"My old man'll hit me! He'll beat me!" Melvin Collins kept yelling, and he started to cry. "He'll beat me because I don't know nuttin'! I git in trouble and I don't know nuttin'!"

It's funny I could hear him while I was yelling at the same time, "You can't bother him! He never wants to be bothered! He won't talk to me! He won't look at me! He doesn't like me!" I guess I was crying too.

The teachers didn't say anything. Miss Mieres stood

there with her hand on the telephone and a funny look on her face. I figured they didn't believe us.

But I believed Melvin Collins. I stopped yelling and looked at him. Even if his face was blurry, I could tell he was looking at me. All I could think was, *His father hits him! His father beats him!*

"Geez," Melvin Collins said. "You know everything, and your dad won't *talk* to you? He won't *look* at you?"

"Hardly ever," I said. "He hates me."

"Geez," he said. And then, "How come you got so mad? So your glasses got broken. I didn't hit you. It's not like when I pushed you in the creek. You didn't yell then. You didn't tell nobody."

"My father said if I broke my glasses again I'd have to go without," I said. "Last time I broke them when I knocked them off the lamp stand because I couldn't see where they were. I can't see anything without them."

"Nuttin'?"

"Well, just a little. I mean, you're all blurry. I can read if I put my nose right on the page."

"Geez," he said again. "You read wit' your nose on the book?"

"Not when I've got my glasses on."

Then he said, "I guess it's no fun bein' smart if your dad won't talk to you."

"I guess it's no fun to get hit," I said.

"Geez, no," he said. Geez."

I thought, he doesn't know very many words to say. But I couldn't think of any either, not just then.

Then Miss Mieres said, "Why did you hit Melvin if you broke your glasses?"

I didn't say anything and neither did Melvin.

Then one of the sixth graders said, "Melvin pulled them off and stamped on them."

I saw Mr. Genovo's arm go up. I heard his hand slap his forehead, and I heard him groan.

Miss Mieres said, "We'll have to tell your father, Melvin. He'll have to pay for new glasses for Ritchie."

Melvin said a word I'd have had my mouth washed out with soap for saying. But he didn't sound mad when he said it. He sounded like he was going to start crying again.

He didn't though and I knew something. I knew he wouldn't go after me again. I even liked him for saying that word out loud. I wished I could have said it. Then I thought some funny things.

I thought, Good-bye, Bratch Bunch Branch. You won't push me around anymore. And I felt pretty good. Then I thought, Okay, all you g. and g.'s, I'll stay home and take care of Rosie, and I felt even better.

Then I thought, And if I can't get the Gornuck to talk to me, I'll just have to cope.

Sixteen

Everybody finally decided Melvin Collins should come home with me and talk to my father. I didn't think *my* father would beat him.

We didn't say anything on the way home. After Mrs. Cavanaugh left, we kind of stood around and waited. I went up and said hi to Rosie and told her she had to wait. I came back down and we waited some more.

Melvin Collins kept looking around the living room. "Geez, a piano!" he said.

"Yeah," I said.

And then, "Geez, all those books!"

"Yeah," I said.

We didn't say much else. I guess Melvin Collins was wondering what I would say to my father.

I was too.

When my father came home at last, I told him, "We were horsing around and my glasses got stepped on and broken."

And Melvin Collins said, "Geez, Mr. Willis, I'm sorry. I'm the one who stepped on them. Geez, I'm sorry."

My father looked sideways at us, the way he does when he looks at me at all. I showed him the bent rims with the glass part gone.

"I suppose it can't be helped," he said in that way that sounds half mad and half in a hurry to get away from me when I'm trying to talk to him. "Tomorrow tell Mrs. Cavanaugh to make an appointment with the eye doctor for you."

Then he walked away from us and went into the kitchen.

Melvin Collins and I stood there. I knew he was staring at me. I was looking at his face too.

"Geez," he said.

"I guess you can go home," I said.

"Yeah. Okay. Yeah. Geez. Thanks. So long, Ritchie."

"So long, Melvin," I said, and opened the door for him.

I went out to the kitchen where my father was warming up the supper.

"Is that the kind of friend you run around with at school?" he asked.

"He's one of them," I said. I forgot to say "Um."

Two days later there was a letter from pod.

> *Dear little rosenander,*
> *Well, as Mother always said, "Look at the black underside of a cloud and you're sure to*

*see lightning." I've not only seen lightning,
but I've heard thunder, too.*

*I heard sloshings early, early yesterday
morning and I hurried to look through the
mailbox hole. I couldn't believe what I saw.
The Gornuck's eye peering back through it
into mine! Jorpaditch help me! (Jorpaditch is a
minor god among the trolls. He helps children.
I still call on him now and again. Habit, I
suppose.) I put my hand over the hole as fast
as I could, and that Gornuck went away—not,
I am sure, because I covered the hole, but
because the sun was coming up.*

*Now that he knows which hole is mine, I'll
have to dig a long tunnel to make a back door
well away from my front door. I must have a
sure way out in case that Big and Slimy
decides to dig out my mailbox hole, sqwooge
in, and break his way through my front
hall.*

*So now I am busy at excavating, a job much
more involved than anyone who doesn't live
halfway underground can understand. In no
way do I want to fill my comfortable living
room with sand and roots and rocks. I have to
start a side tunnel from the outside so that I
can push the debris from the main tunnel into
the creek until I break through into my pantry.
It's from there that I'll tunnel through to an
escape door, always carrying the dirt farther*

and farther from the longer tunnel to the creek.

The back door can't come out near the culvert by the road, because if the creek floods, the culvert will be full and my tunnel could easily flood too (I don't have time to waterproof it). Then my house would flood. It will have to open on the other side of the orchard near the house where the Man and that yappy little dog live. That's much too close for my comfort, but it will also be much, much too close for the Gornuck's. I hope he would not dare come that near the Man. All of these considerations leave me dizzy.

It is *frightful* that there are some who think they have to have what belongs to someone else, or make slaves of them in the kitchen. What is the matter with the creatures of this world? Unfeeling! So many of them like the Bratch Bunch Branch! And to try to *talk* to them! Almost impossible! But I will try to talk to the Gornuck somehow. He *should* listen to reason. Shouldn't everybody?

Oh, I don't want to bother your young heads with questions I'm not wise enough to answer myself. I hope I haven't distressed you. I still have a lot more brain than the Gornuck, and believe me, I'll use it!

I just hope that my next letter to you will be filled with happy news. In fact, I am *sure* there

will be some. You know how people gossip?
Well, every now and then when I'm hiding
behind the onion sacks in Kulich's corner
store, I hear some. I have just heard a lovely
rumor. I only want to be absolutely certain it's
true before I tell you what it is.

As ever,
your truthful pod

p.s. I understand Ritchie has settled things
with Melvin Collins. The direct approach.
"Slam, crash! A fine way!" as Mother says. I'm
not so sure it's a fine way, but maybe
sometimes it's the only way, and I'm so glad
it's done with!

There was a lot I thought about in that letter.
I helped Rosie write again, after "Dear pod," one letter
at a time:

> *Dear pod. Put the dirt in your mailbox*
> *hallway. I still love you. rosenander.*

I left it under the rock.
Three days later there was another letter from pod. I
read it to Rosie:

> *Dear rosenander,*
> *I took your advice to put the dirt in my*
> *front hallway, and I am so glad I did! The*
> *Gornuck is steadily digging through it, but I*
> *know it has slowed him down.*

*There is also good news. I have almost
broken through into the orchard. I was outside
early in the morning to check my course when
that noisy little dog saw me and came running.
I had to climb a tree. She yapped and yapped
and yapped. Finally the Man came out. He
came right to the edge of the orchard.*

"Is anybody there?" he shouted.

*Of course I held my breath and didn't say
a word! That little krinkaw snuffled and
scratched and whined just where I thought the
opening should be. Finally the Man called it
off. He sounded very irritated. I was irritated
too!*

*But all that is in the past. Now I only need
to pack a few belongings in my knapsack, and
if I can just break through into the orchard
before the Gornuck breaks through into my
living room, I'll be away from both these
wretched creatures forever. I'll leave at an
hour when the Man is sure to have that dog
shut up in his house. That's the good news.*

*The even better news is this. The rumor is
true. Your mother will be home with you a
week from Friday! Take good care of her.*

When I read that, I got so excited my lips got numb.
Rosie's mouth fell open and her eyes got huge. I whispered the rest of it:

Yours, ever faithful and honest, pod

p.s. Thank you a thousand troll thanks for your
letter! I would have leaped out of my shoes with
joy if I hadn't been so stiff from digging.
p.p.s. I am sending you a little package. I don't
have room for it in my knapsack and I
don't want the Gornuck finding it."

Seventeen

Rosie and I didn't know what to yell about first. Pod was almost safe and our mother was coming home! We yelled and whooped and danced around until she got tired and had to lie down.

I knew one thing I would do absolutely for sure. I'd ask my father. All he would have to say was yes or no.

So after supper, I asked.

"Will our mother be home a week from Friday?"

He looked at me, surprised. "Yes," he said.

I waited for him to ask me how I knew, but he didn't. All of a sudden I thought, it's not my fault! He just doesn't know how, and he never will. He won't be any different whatever I do. I'll just have to cope.

I knew something else, too. No matter what my father said, tomorrow I would tell Thad Grailowsky that our mother would be home. I wouldn't bother him. I wouldn't stay and visit. I'd just knock on the door and tell him and then go home.

Friday I stopped at his house after school, but he wasn't home. Pooch was on the back steps and she let me pet her and play tug of war with an old sock. She growled and shook and pulled and so did I. When I went home through the field, she watched me go, but she didn't follow me.

There was snow on the ground and I made footsteps where the path should be. I didn't care who saw them.

After Rosie and I got over talking about our mother coming home, we began wondering about pod again. What was he sending to Rosie? Did he really get away? Was he gone? Would he ever write again?

On Saturday morning I went over to Thad Grailow-sky's. Of course I went in the house. He had to close the door so the cold wouldn't come in while I told him our mother would be coming home next Friday.

"Hey, Ritchie! That's *great*!" he said, and swung me around in the air. He was just as glad about it as I was!

Then I saw that he was packing stuff up.

"You going someplace?" I asked.

"Yeah," he said. "Away."

"Why?" I asked. "Where?"

He waved a hand at a newspaper. It was an old paper from way back in September. The headlines were about Hitler invading Poland and burning Warsaw. "I'm going to fight."

"We're not in that war," I told him.

"I'm joining the Canadian Army," he said.

• • •

When I got home, the mailman had brought a little package for Rosie. There was a stone in it with a letter wrapped all around it.

She held the stone and I read her the letter:

Toltroddy

Dear rosenander,

This is a rare-green-flat-round-creek pebble. It is one of the last two that I have. I won't need any where I am going, but I am keeping one to be a reminder of here, my home, for so many thousands of years.

It will also remind me of you because these are what I used to pay for the paper I bought in Kulich's corner store so I could write letters to you. Of course I would never forget you anyway, but it will comfort me to have something I can hold in my hand when I am worried or frightened. The minute I touch it, I will say to myself, rosenander! She cared about me and helped me through a dreadful time. That will make me feel warm and happy and brave. I will never feel so small and insignificant and ineffectual again.

I am sending the other one to you now because I don't want the Gornuck to have it and I'll be too busy to send it on the last day I am here.

By the way, that Gornuck does have sharp teeth! I saw them from my bedroom window

*last night while he was scratching and digging
and grinning to himself.*

"Grinning!" Rosie cried. "He's awful! Keep reading."
I nodded and swallowed.

> *I shall be so glad to be away from him. And
> now that I've thought it over, I don't think he
> would have eaten Ritchie when he fell into
> the creek. I know for certain he's afraid of
> people and won't have anything to do with
> them. He swims away very quickly and quietly
> if any member of Homo sapiens happens by
> on an evening stroll. You won't have to worry
> about him, but I have been very frightened.
> Having your letters was the best way in the
> world to help me cope with fear, loneliness,
> and despair.*
>
> *Thank you forever.*
>
> *Now I must go and dig some more. I hope
> you will remember that I will always be your
> friend. I know you wish me good luck because
> you are my friend too.*
>
>> *porolli doumuob illoroq, troll.*
>> *otherwise known as pod*

> *p.s.: Just for something else to remember me
> by, here are the names of troll days: Schrodol,
> Salictort, Mokrits, Thanderol, Wilkeron,
> Toltroddy, Moskanipi, and Finipid. As you see,
> we have eight days in a week. It makes it*

impossible to figure out which one is which of
your days.
p.p.s.: Remember to wash your face and brush
your teeth every night and morning. As
Mother always says, A clean face is a sweet
greeting, and brushed bicuspids bite better.

Those were the last words.

I finished the letter just when we heard our father's car come into the driveway.

Rosie let me hold the stone for a minute. It was smooth and flat and cool. Then she wanted it back. She curled her fingers tight around it. "Poor pod!" she said, and her underlip came out. "He's been so scared." She cried and I hugged her.

"He'll be all right," I said. Oh, how I hoped he got away! But how would we ever know if we didn't get a letter?

For the next three days we kept telling each other that pod was all right, but of course we weren't sure. Then a postcard with a picture of the lions in front of the Art Institute on it came from Chicago.

The note said:

Had great luck hitching a ride in the back
of a big moving van full of furniture. Am
doing all right and am very excited about the
trip. love, honest pod.

Rosie cried again.

Two days later a letter came.

Dear rosenander,

    I'm still in Chicago.

    You should hear what it sounds like under the els! I never realized what troll music was! I've had to make do with the natural sounds of the river and birds and the noises the Man made that you call music. But the noise of trains over a bridge or on an elevated track . . . that is real music! Troll music! I do believe I am finding my true self!

    A real troll in spite of my size!

    So, off to South America!

                          love, pod

This time we both laughed.

Then Friday came at last. Pod was right. Did he really know from listening to gossip in Kulich's corner store? *I* never heard gossip there. But where else would he have heard it? Maybe that was where Thad Grailowsky heard things too. If it was, I was glad they heard it, because they told me things nobody else ever did.

Now they were both gone, but our mother came home. Our father brought her in the car.

Eighteen

We couldn't stop hugging our mother for a long time. Then we talked. We sat in the kitchen so we wouldn't bother our father, but a couple of times he came out and listened. She told us how she was in a hospital in another town and how glad she was to get our letter. We talked about all kinds of things until she was tired and had to rest.

Only we didn't tell her about pod's letters. We wanted to, but Rosie and I had talked it over and decided it would be better to wait a while. Maybe until pod told us we could. But of course we couldn't ask him. He wasn't there for us to leave him a letter.

By Christmastime things were almost the same as they used to be. Rosie was out of bed all day, except for a nap in the afternoon. Our mother had a nap then too. Our mother baked good pies and read to Rosie in the evenings just like she always did.

But some things were different from before. Pearl Suslik came three mornings a week and did the breakfast dishes and made beds. Mrs. Cavanaugh came twice a week and did the ironing and the big cleaning. And after New Year's, Rosie started morning kindergarten.

By Valentine's Day that awful time when our mother was gone and Rosie was sick was all shrinking away like a bad dream—except for pod. The only thing real about it were his letters. I'd still read them to Rosie on Saturday mornings when our mother and father went out to do the big shopping. And we kept watching the mailbox. The letters we had had truly come in the mail. We'd look at the envelopes to make sure. The postmarks were real.

Then one day, it was a Friday—Rosie insisted it was Moskinipi—did everything always happen on Fridays? Our mother changed the paper in Rosie's chest of drawers. Saturday morning we both knew because Rosie's understuff and stockings and garter vests were all straightened out and the greasy spot where Rosie had put cookies one time was gone. Of course, Mrs. Cavanaugh had been there to do the cleaning, but she never changed the papers in the drawers. We knew our mother had done it.

When Rosie opened the drawer and we saw it all that way—neat and clean—I almost stopped breathing. But the letters were still there, under the paper. There was no way of telling if our mother had read any of them. But of course she knew they were there.

Saturday afternoon we brought them to the kitchen table and the three of us sat there while Rosie handed them to our mother to read, one by one, in order.

There were nine letters and a postcard. She read them all out loud.

Then she asked, "Do you know who wrote them?"

Of course Rosie said, "Pod did!"

But our mother was really asking me.

I shook my head no. All at once I thought of something I'd never thought of before. It made me stare at her. "Did *you*?"

"No," she said.

Of course I knew right away she couldn't have, because except for the Chicago ones, they were postmarked from our own town. But she had a funny look on her face and she shook her head, as if she thought maybe she knew. She had a wondering look on her face, and sad, too, and all kinds of I-don't-know-what showed. A kind of look like the way music makes me feel.

Then she smiled, and said, "Well, I guess we'll all just have to say that Rosie is right. A very kind pod wrote them to keep you from being lonesome."

"Kind pod? *He* was lonesome!" Rosie cried. "He wanted a friend. He wanted *me*. He *needed* me! I was his *friend*! I made him happy!"

"Of course you did!" Our mother hugged Rosie hard. Then she hugged me. She had her eyes closed. I thought she might almost want to cry, but grown-ups don't cry, and why should she, anyway? She said, "Why don't you put the letters back in your drawer, Rosie."

So Rosie did.

One day, a while later, a postcard came from Toronto, Canada. It said:

I can't belive it! I took the wrong train!
What a ridiculous way to get to the Peruvian
Andes! pod

"It sure is," I shouted, and Rosie and I grabbed hands and laughed and swung around in a circle until she was so dizzy we both fell down.

Quite a long time later Rosie had one more letter. It came from London, England.

SCHRODOL

Dear rosenander,

You can't believe the world over here—the
other side of the world from where I was
trying to go! But the fascinating thing is that I
have met several other small, ineffectual,
insignificant ones of my kind. They're all
much concerned about what people—Homo
sapiens—are doing to one another and have
decided to form a coalition of trolls to infiltrate
and—oh, I mustn't give away any secrets.
They would just get censored anyway. But I
have decided to join them.

I will say the stakes are very high. In fact,
they are the highest they ever are when it
comes to this sort of thing. Of course, we don't
know how it will all turn out, but we believe
we have chosen the right side.

I've heard nothing but dreadful rumors
about the Bratch Bunch Branch. They are

definitely on the other side. Well, what must be
must be. We shall do our best. When it is over,
I shall certainly find my way to Mother and
Father and all the g. and g's.
    I send you all my love.
        Yours for forever and a day, pod.

There was no p.s.

It was the last letter Rosie had from him.

We missed having them, but with our mother home, we didn't seem to need pod's letters as much. Rosie and I did talk about him for quite a while. We wondered where he was and how all those great-g. and -g.'s were getting along. Rosie would tell me what *she* thought he was doing and where he was. She said he had done everything he could in England, so he crossed the ocean to South America where he was safe from the big war with all the bombings and other scary stuff that was going on. He was having adventures and keeping everybody cheered up, the way he'd cheered us up.

I helped her find all the countries in South America on the globe until she knew them by heart. Then I helped her find new places for him to go where it was safe. She could find them all on the globe anytime, even when our father was home, because our mother said she could. Sometimes, when our mother helped us out with where pod might be, our father didn't even say we were making too much noise.

I didn't know whether he knew we were pretending things. Maybe he did, because sometimes he was in the room when Rosie asked for a big troll hand to help her. I didn't care so much if he did know. We liked to do it. And if we had to cope, maybe our mother told him he had to cope too.

When Rosie was six years old, our mother gave her a little box of dark brown wood, all smooth and polished. It was just the right size and had a lid that locked with a key. The lid had a face carved in it. It could have been a troll's face.

Our father asked, "What kind of a present is that for a kid?"

"Little girls like boxes to keep things in," our mother told him.

"Um," he said, without opening his mouth.

Melvin Collins didn't bother me at school anymore. We almost got to be friends. I mean, there was never anything much we had to talk about with each other because what he did and what I did were so different. Besides, in another year we were in junior high and didn't have any of the same classes together. But we always nodded if we saw each other in the hallway. It was sort of knowing something we both had the same, and it was a good feeling.

Then one Sunday afternoon in December—it was more than two years since pod's letters came—we were home listening to the radio. Artur Rubinstein was playing a Brahms piano concerto with the New York Philharmonic. News kept breaking into the concert.

136

We were in the war.

When that happened, all the factories were in the war effort and everybody was working all the time. The factory that used to make cars tested airplane engines now. You could hear them humming all day and all night. My father worked at the office from early to late because they were in the war effort too. He was always tired, so our mother told us to keep quiet when he was home. He didn't talk to us any more than he ever had. We didn't have to get used to that. But I got to wondering if he thought about anything but work. Sometimes I wondered what he liked. Maybe he told my mother at night after we went to bed. But he never told us, so I guessed I would never know. I decided I wouldn't be that way when I grew up.

Mrs. Cavanaugh and Pearl Suslik both worked on the assembly line in a factory. Rosie and I had to help with the housework. We practiced the piano, too. In the winter we practiced with our coats on because we didn't warm the living room up very much on account of saving fuel because of the war.

Our mother practiced with her coat on too. She kept track of the rationing stamps for shoes and meat and butter and sugar and gas for the car, and did volunteer work. Sometimes she played concerts for sailors from the Great Lakes Naval Training Station and soldiers from Fort Sheridan.

Sometimes she took us into Chicago on the North Shore train to hear the Chicago Symphony Orchestra. I recognized the man who had played second violin with Thad

Grailowsky. His hair was white now instead of gray and he sat in the first violin section. On the program it said his name was Hugh Wegner. I didn't see the others—the quartet's first violin or the viola. Maybe they were in the war.

When we were sophomores in high school, Melvin Collins dropped out and joined the navy. He lied about how old he was—he was really only sixteen, but he was big and got away with it.

With the war and everything, I almost forgot about pod. I certainly didn't bother to wonder who he was anymore. And Rosie didn't talk about him. She could read his letters herself if she wanted to.

But I never forgot Thad Grailowsky. His shack was always there to remind me. New people, Mr. and Mrs. Roddy, had moved in when he left. They took care of Pooch, but they both worked so I never got to know them very well. I'd stop after school and pet Pooch and play with her. Afterward I'd walk home through the field. It kept the grass from growing over the path.

There was always news about our Army and Navy and Air Corps and Marines. There were names of places— Bataan and Guadalcanal and Iwo Jima. There was news about bombings, and the Russians asking for a second front. There was news about North Africa. Then there was D-day and our soldiers landing in Normandy. When that happened, I came home from school at noon and told my mother about it, and she cried.

Grown-ups did cry.

There was always all that news about us, but I wished

we had more news about Canada. I always wondered where the Canadian Army was.

One day I came home from school and there was a car with Illinois license plates on it. We didn't see cars from Chicago so much because of gas rationing, but I recognized this one. It was the one that used to be parked outside Thad Grailowsky's shack.

I recognized the second violinist too—the one from the quartet that day. He and my mother were sitting at the kitchen table and my mother looked sick. He stood up when I came in.

"Hello, Ritchie," he said. "Do you remember me?" and held out his hand.

"Sure, Mr. Wegner," I told him, and shook his hand. I was glad I'd found his name in the symphony program and remembered it.

"I was just leaving," he said, and then he said to our mother, "It's not certain."

She sort of nodded and stood up and went to the door with Mr. Wegner.

"Thank you," she said.

"He asked me—if anything happened—to let you know. I didn't just want to write," Mr. Wegner said.

Our mother nodded again, and said "Thank you" again.

When he was gone, our mother said to me, "It's Thad Grailowsky. He's missing in action."

Then she went upstairs.

I didn't know how to feel. Just empty. I went into the living room and sat down at the piano, but I didn't want to play anything. I walked around and thought about him. I thought about Blackie and the peanut butter sandwich. I thought about his voice that was strong and warm and how his tongue made sort of *dh* out of *d*, and what a nice sound it was. I thought of how the cello sang when he played it. I thought about how his hands were strong and warm too when they grabbed my wrists and pulled me out of the creek. I thought about people who had to kill other people because they wanted to run the world. I thought how stupid it was for anybody to want to run the world, and how hard it was to stop them.

At last there was V-E day and the atom bomb and V-J day. The war was over, and everybody was laughing and screaming and hugging one another.

Then one day Rosie brought in the mail. She began to yell and jump up and down.

I said before it was the last *letter* Rosie ever got. This was a postcard. There wasn't any return address—not even T.U.B. And the writing—I mean printing—wasn't the same, all neat and easy to read. It was sort of a scrawl. Besides Rosie's name and our address, there were just two words:

We won. And underneath, *pod*.

Rosie showed it to our mother, and our mother began to laugh. Then I saw tears in her eyes when she was hugging Rosie.

I looked at the postcard again. It was postmarked from England.

I'd be a senior in high school pretty soon. I knew pod would never be back, but all at once I knew Thad Grailowsky wasn't missing anymore. He would come home some day.